Bridge of Sighs

ALSO BY PAULETTE ROESKE

POETRY

Anvil, Clock & Last

Divine Attention

The Body Can Ascend No Higher

Breathing Under Water

Bridge of Sighs

A NOVELLA AND STORIES

Paulette Roeske

Story Line Press
Ashland, Oregon

PS
3568
.O367
B75
2002

Copyright © 2002 by Paulette Roeske

First Printing

All rights reserved. No part of this book may be reproduced in any form or by any electronic or mechanical means, including information storage and retrieval systems, without permission in writing from the publisher except for brief quotations in a critical article or review.

Published by Story Line Press, Three Oaks Farm, PO Box 1240, Ashland, OR 97520-0055.

www.storylinepress.com

This publication was made possible thanks in part to the generous support of the Nicholas Roerich Museum, the Andrew W. Mellon Foundation, the National Endowment for the Arts, and our individual contributors.

Cover design by Lysa McDowell
Cover art by Dan Ziembo
Interior design by Valerie Brewster, Scribe Typography

LIBRARY OF CONGRESS CATALOGING-IN-PUBLICATION DATA

Roeske, Paulette
Bridge of sighs: a novella and stories / by Paulette Roeske.
p. cm.
ISBN 1-58654-019-X
1. Americans—Italy—Fiction. 2. Loss (Psychology)—Fiction. 3. Women—Italy—Fiction. 4. Italy—Fiction. I. Title.
PS3568.O367 B75 2002
813'.54—DC21   2002007752

This is a work of fiction. Names, characters, places, and incidents in this book are the product of the author's imagination or are used fictitiously. Any similarity to real persons and events is coincidental and not intended by the author.

*For my husband, Robert,
and all fellow travelers*

ACKNOWLEDGMENTS

The author gratefully acknowledges the editors of the following journals in which the following stories first appeared, sometimes in different forms: *Glimmer Train:* "The Hard Fact"; *Louisiana Literature:* "Smaller Than Life"; *Other Voices:* "A History of Swimming"; *The Short Fiction Review:* "Four Characters, Three Small Stories"; *The Short Story Review:* "From This Distance."

The author also wishes to thank the Illinois Arts Council, Ragdale Foundation, and the College of Lake County for support during the time some of these stories were written.

Special thanks are due Story Line Press, particularly Robert McDowell and the judges for the Three Oaks Prize in Fiction.

Lisel Mueller, John Van Doren, Stuart Dybek, Patricia Aakhus, Larry Starzec, Neal Lulofs, and Noah Lukeman read the manuscript with care and offered encouragement and selfless counsel. To each of them I am deeply grateful.

Contents

FROM THIS DISTANCE
3

OPEN ARMS
11

THE HARD FACT
25

SMALLER THAN LIFE
39

A HISTORY OF SWIMMING
45

FOUR CHARACTERS,
THREE SMALL STORIES
53

THE ECSTASY
OF MAGDA BRUMMEL
57

I stood in Venice on the Bridge of Sighs,
A palace and a prison on each hand . . .
LORD BYRON
from *Childe Harold's Pilgrimage*

Bridge of Sighs

From This Distance

WHEN THE WOMAN BOARDS THE BUS THERE IS ONE seat left. Believing it is meant for her, she slips into it like a hand into a pocket. The bus will cross three time zones before it reaches its destination, but not everyone travels such a distance. Because the seats are oversold, those who board later will have to stand. In this way some passengers will come to think themselves lucky, others unlucky.

When she takes her seat beside him, the sleeping man is unaware how subtly her body replaces the air. Propped against the window is a pillow in a floral case on which the old man rests his head. If the woman cared to look out the window, her view would be a perpetual meadow.

The man has hooked his cane over the back of the seat in front of him and lined the window ledge with crackers in cellophane packets, Styrofoam cups, and stacks of bottle caps. One hand wrapped in a dirty kerchief rests on his belly like a paw. The woman stores her satchel beneath her seat. From her purse she removes a copy of *The Lives of the Saints*. She lays it on top of the purse in her lap and begins to read the story of St. Roch, venerable saint of invalids, who survived the forest by eating bread brought to him in the mouths of dogs.

No armrest separates the two seats, and when the man shifts his great weight in his sleep he edges past the invisible barrier between his body and hers. The woman keeps her arms tight against her sides and tries to turn the pages by moving only her wrists. She leans toward the aisle, pressing into the metal arm that cuts beneath her ribs. She recognizes the pain as the kind brought on by running too far or too fast.

Once the woman rode a bus to the interior of an island in the tropics. She was young then. Then, as now, the bus could not accommodate all those who wished to travel. But still they boarded — men carrying whole stalks of bananas, women subduing runty chickens or dragging baskets they would later balance on their heads. Others clung to the exterior like lichen. The woman stood in the aisle among them, their unwashed bodies rubbing hers, their weight on her when the bus swerved to avoid fallen rocks or goats grazing in the garbage beside the one-lane road that curled up the mountain like smoke. She held her arms across her breasts in a small gesture of protection. When the bus veered close to the mountain's edge, she shut her eyes and imagined herself making the sign of the cross.

Standing in the aisle beside her is a Mexican man, a migrant worker, the woman thinks, traveling in the wrong direction. She imagines his despair when he confronts a city of brick and stone, the unrelenting rows of tall buildings. What will he do there, after his seamless years in the vast groves of oranges, fruit waiting for his hand? Beginning in the middle, she thinks, with no guiding edge, no coast to foster correction, poses the opportunity for such an error. The hem of the man's jacket brushes across the woman's face when he ducks from left to right to glimpse the prairie slipping by. The fabric smells rich, dark, like dirt.

Without warning the old man leans toward the woman as if to confide in her. She leans into the Mexican. Glancing up, she cannot read the expression on his face. He may as well be deaf and dumb. Abruptly the old man shifts again and rests his forehead against the back of the seat in front of him. He doesn't move for a long time. When he finally settles back into his seat, he says, "Sometimes I have to sit like that. I had an operation on my spine. The doc he cut some bone out of my leg and put it in my spine." He bends over and tries to pull up his pant leg to show the woman the scar, but the effort is too great.

At great expense the woman traveled to the island to marry. Her lover had been born in a tin-roofed house on a mountain, he told her, where sugar cane in the front yard grew taller than most men. As a boy he climbed to the top of the mango tree and from that distance commanded a view of the sea. At age thirty he sailed, leaving behind his good family name. In America he longed for the sound of rain pricking the tin roof, the sweet cane, his mountain, and the promises of the sea. When the longing grew too great to bear, he returned to the island. He sent for the woman. By the time she arrived, his charming English was laced with patois.

"Let me tell you something," the old man says, turning toward the woman. "This happened back in Omaha. A man with one leg sat right where you're sitting. I helped him off at the lunch stop." The woman listens but doesn't look up from her book. She marks her place by holding one finger beside St. Sebastian.

"In the diner I sat next to him. Like friends. After a while he hitches his crutches under his arms and says he's going to the toilet. 'Better forget it,' I tell him. We was punching a time clock, you see." The man wipes his rheumy eyes without unwrapping the kerchief tied around his hand. "I'm damned if that driver didn't take no head count."

The woman wonders how long ago Omaha was and where the man with one leg is now. "You didn't tell the driver?" she asks at last.

"I let people make their own mistakes," says the old man, settling back in his seat and closing his eyes.

"Please," the woman said. "Please," she repeated, threading her way between bodies, stalks of bananas, baskets spilling their odors of fish and flower into air so thick it propelled her like a hand at her back. When at last she stood on solid ground, she fingered the rosary in her pocket.

The stop was unmarked by town, shelter, or sign. Unmet, the woman could think of nothing to do except listen to the reluctant engine grow fainter. The sun burned her hair, her scalp, burned deeper into her brain until the neon palms and red bottlebrush trees swirled like a kaleidoscope.

Three naked boys darted out of the brush swinging bunches of dull berries with thick, wrinkled skins they had picked from the bushes beside the road where they grew unchecked. These, she understood, they wanted her to buy. The boys danced in a circle around her. *Little monkeys*, she thought. She opened her purse and gave each an American dollar. They ran off, waving the bills like flags. The woman sat down on her suitcase and split open one of the berries with her fingers. The flesh was green, translucent, and bitter.

Because she was already halfway up the mountain, the woman began to walk. Soon the road became even less of a road. Steep, rutted, it threatened to topple her, and the weight of her suitcase pulled her off balance. Although she could see no one in any direction, she pushed through the thick bushes using her suitcase as a shield. Removing her shoes and pantyhose, she squatted to relieve herself. Afterward, she wriggled out of her slip without taking off her dress. She hung the slip on a branch, and behind it she secured her hose so the feet nearly touched the ground. She left her shoes beneath the hose, side by side, as if they were waiting for someone else to step into them. Barefoot, she walked more easily. Each step raised a cloud of dust finer than sand, but when she looked back she saw that a light breeze had already erased her footprints.

She heard the engine before she saw the car, a Volkswagen wildly painted over every inch that was not rusted through. The driver stopped but left the engine running. When he opened his mouth to call to her, she saw nearly all his teeth were gold. He leaned across the seat and flipped open the door, motioning broadly as if she were simple-minded. When she hoisted her suitcase inside, the driver sped away. The open door swung to breaking as the car took the curve. Inside the suitcase was a wedding dress of pale yellow linen, five white cotton nightgowns, and pastel shifts suited to the tropics, all newly purchased, layered in tissue, and punctuated with satin roses filled with sachet. The driver would find them when he forced the lock.

The road never branched, but gradually it narrowed until it became a path that the woman followed until it stopped at a thick wall of foliage. Behind it sprawled a pink stucco house with a roof that glinted like the sea. Wild parrots scolded from the mango tree where they were perched, and through the waving cane she glimpsed the man himself. He sat on the veranda in a rattan chair he balanced on its two back legs. Crossed at the ankles, his feet rested on the white wrought-iron railing. Although his safari hat was pulled low over his eyes, he was not asleep. He did not move until she stood before him, and even then he did not rise.

The old man unwraps the kerchief from his hand, revealing nothing more than the ordinary mate to the other. He pulls a newspaper from the duffel bag at his feet. From the window ledge he selects three bottle caps from the bottom of the stack and lines them up on the newspaper. Slipping a dried pea under the one in the center, he begins moving the caps with a dexterity that attracts the woman. The ropy blue veins and liver spots on his hands blur as the little red caps flash beneath his fingers like promises.

He begins to talk about tolls, how they have risen. Because of his age and his habit of travel, he knows the history of tolls. "Used to be five cents would get you through," he says. "Now you'll pay ninety-five, and what can you do about it? Turn around? Yep, they got you all right."

His hands gradually slow, like a train pulling into a station. "Can you guess where the pea is hiding?" the man asks coyly, without taking his eyes from his hands.

The woman looks past him at the pillow propped against the window. There is an oily stain in the shape of the man's head on the flowered case.

"No harm in taking a guess," he urges. "You got nothing but time to kill."

The woman doesn't answer.

"This one?" he asks again, poising a finger above the cap closest to her. Pointing to each of the others, he repeats his question. Quickly he reshuffles the caps. His voice resumes its two-beat measure. *This one? This one?*

Finally she nods.

"You got a sharp eye, little miss," he says. "Yep, you're a lucky one."

Somehow the woman feels grateful for this chance to be right, as if being right this time could cancel a history of wrong choices. Each time the man asks, the woman chooses correctly. This part of her journey seems familiar, the simple triumph for which she has spent her life preparing. She searches her memory for the name of an appropriate saint to thank.

"Now how about a little wager?" the man asks, "just to sweeten the pot. When you get to where you're going you treat yourself to a night on the town. You'll be thanking me."

The woman stops suddenly, as if she has come to the edge of a great precipice. Deep in her pocket the smooth crystal beads of her rosary lie coiled. Beside it are five President Jacksons, all gazing in the man's direction. She stares past the bottle caps at the newspaper headlines announcing week-old tragedies.

"Come now, Lady Luck won't wait all day," he says impatiently.

The woman slips her hand into her pocket and lets her fingers close over the top bill. For a moment her hand hovers at the rim of her pocket, and then she asks, "Where shall I put it?"

A few minutes later the old man folds all five bills into his palm and wraps the soiled kerchief around it like a bandage. He drops the rosary into the duffel bag still open on the floor between his legs. "Lady Luck closed her eyes on you, little miss," he says, leaning back against his pillow.

Everything her lover had told her about the island was true, but he had not told her everything. Through the wrought-iron grillwork barring the windows, the woman watched a shadow move from room to room. She put her hand on the man's hand as she had done when they worked side by side in the laboratory at the famous midwestern university where they had met. His white cuff stopped sharply at his wrist; against his brown skin, it was like a line someone dared you to cross. But how could he have resisted the music of her splayed fingers tapping the back of his hand; and she, how long could she continue calling Christ her only bridegroom?

A mulatto girl of fourteen came out onto the veranda through a set of double doors; the man shifted in his chair, displacing the woman's hand. With a broom fashioned from stalks of dried cane, the girl jabbed at a lizard that was almost invisible against the speckled tile. One night at a time she had moved her clothes from the tiny servant's room off the kitchen to the big bedroom with double doors opening onto the veranda. The man had taken the room after the deaths of his parents during the year the woman had required to arrange her journey. On the island they were already calling the man *massa*. The girl swept up every petal, every grain of sand. Little by little the woman understood that the girl swept with an air of propriety.

Anticipating her stop, the woman rises, puts *The Lives of the Saints* on her seat, and reaches for her satchel. Before she can retrieve it, the old man shifts into her place.

"Please," says the woman.

"Now let me out. I got things to do."

"Please," she repeats.

The man unhooks his cane from the back of the seat. Swinging the crook, he knocks his pillow to the floor and scatters his collection of crackers, cups, and bottle caps. He jabs at the woman with the tip of his cane but strikes the Mexican who has no room to move. Elbows akimbo, the woman fends off both men as she drags her satchel from beneath the seat. When the old man jabs again, the Mexican catches the cane and wrenches it from his grasp. Reaching under the old man's haunches with both hands, the woman pulls her book free. He topples against the window, striking his head against the glass and thrashing his arms and legs like an upturned beetle.

The woman pushes past the Mexican who has stood for hours without complaint but now will not be distracted from the empty seat. He moves in, filling the space like a river suddenly diverted.

"Spick!" shouts the old man, "Whore!" He wets himself with the effort of his struggle.

"*No hablo Ingles*," says the Mexican, shrugging.

No other passenger turns to help.

If the old man were to look back through the window of the departing bus, he would see the woman standing with her satchel, her purse, and her book on the edge of the flat prairie town where no one waits to meet her. He would see her become smaller.

As for the woman, she watches the bus disappear like a ship over the horizon while silently mouthing the last prayer that will ever cross her lips. The next day the old man will point to the mark on his forehead and tell his story to whoever has the luck to sit beside him.

Open Arms

LIZ AND TONY ENDED UP LIVING TOGETHER BY accident. If it hadn't been for the fire, he would still be living in his apartment and she would be welcoming him with open arms on weekends when he stayed with her. That had been their arrangement for seven years. Then her life had had order, a design as simple and perfect as the white cameos on the Wedgwood stored in padded cases in her bottom dresser drawer.

Before the fire, on weekdays when she woke alone, she had stretched and lain in bed listening to *Earl Grant, Live at the Organ,* her favorite tape. After the fire Tony complained, "Nobody listens to this stuff." He said this even though she explained she had studied organ as a girl and even won first place on a locally televised talent show for her interpretation of "Ebb Tide."

"If I wouldn't have quit, I'd be where Earl Grant is today," she told Tony, recalling with sudden longing those mornings she had spent imagining Earl's slender fingers flashing up and down the keyboard, seeing in his liquid arpeggios whole flocks of shore birds chased by wind-tossed waves.

The evening of the fire she had grilled Tony's steak just the way he liked it, charred outside but bloody when he pierced it with his fork. After dinner they'd gone to a movie, and then to bed. Lying beside Tony, she felt protected, safe, the way she had before Sonny-love-of-her-life left her for a woman young enough to be his daughter who, he had intimated, held a hush-hush position with the CIA. No matter what Sonny said, Liz knew just what position that was.

Nestled deep under the blankets and down comforter, she and Tony talked about marriage, about the son who would inherit her dark curls and green eyes and his olive complexion and muscular build. In Tony's mind the boy looked like Mr. America, but for her the baby gradually turned into a girl. They had been making love when the telephone rang. When he returned four hours later, nearly everything he owned was gone.

Liz smelled Tony before he actually entered her apartment. The whiff of smoke that seeped past the closed door hit her full force when she opened it. He stood in the hall with an olive drab duffel bag at his feet. Over his arm he held a bulky winter jacket with a fake fur border around the hood. She thought he looked like a trapper returned from a bad hunt.

Tony didn't say anything. He stepped into the entry, dumped his jacket on the floor beside the coat rack, and stooped to unlace his boots. The laces were crisscrossed in a complicated pattern he had learned during his hitch in the army a decade ago. The boots were wet and dirty. She stood over him, waiting for him to finish. When he got the right one off, she picked it up by the tongue and set it out in the hall. She put the left one out after it and inspected the pale blue Chinese rug that no shoe had ever touched, as she had repeatedly reminded him.

Tony straightened up. "Well," he began, "guess I'll be staying a few days."

A rush of sympathy for Tony competed with her concern about the rug. Should she pull him close or put him in the tub and bathe him?

"How about a shower?" she asked.

Hearing the water run, she went into the bathroom, gathered up his underwear, denim shirt, and jeans, and took them down to the basement laundry room. She spun the dials to hot wash/hot rinse and tossed in an extra measure of detergent. Her quarters fell with consecutive clicks and the machine started up.

When she opened the door to her apartment, she exhaled sharply, as if to blow back smoke's frilled curtain that her senses had somehow forgotten in the few minutes she'd spent downstairs. Breathing through her mouth, she emptied from the duffel bag what Tony had salvaged: two twenty-five pound dumbbells, the grip exercisers he worked while watching television, a pair of bronze bookends—busts of Abraham Lincoln. She picked up the bag. If she hurried, she could add it to the load. On her way out the door, she removed Tony's jacket from the hook and laid it in the hall next to his boots. Once he had offered her a pair of cast-offs, she suddenly remembered, to keep outside her door so people in the building wouldn't think she was a woman alone. He had put it like that—a woman alone.

The next morning Liz woke to a series of little squeaks she confused with a dream she'd been having about a boat chained to a dock. When she opened her eyes she saw Tony sitting on the edge of the bed in his pajama bottoms, working his grip exercisers. Each time he squeezed the spring-loaded handles, they squeaked. As soon as she grew accustomed to the predictable rhythm, he changed to a pattern of longs and shorts that sounded like Morse code, a message she could not decipher. She snapped Earl Grant into the tape deck on the nightstand. That's when Tony started to complain.

After breakfast he took her to see his apartment. Sheets of plywood stamped ANCHOR BOARD-UP quickly identified his windows in the yellow brick high-rise. The soot-ringed frames looked like giant targets. Tony's name had turned up in the bull's-eye when fate's flaming arrow struck. On the sixth floor, Tony unlocked the door that opened onto the kitchen where the fire had started. The light from the hall illuminated the gas stove, which had been pushed into the middle of the room, its lines disconnected. A large hole gaped behind it. The explosion had blown the cabinets off the walls and the floor was littered with broken glass. Liz kept thinking some martyr might like to walk barefoot across it, every step a matter of mortification and ecstasy. Among the shards she recognized the dishes she had given Tony, brown melamine with a bouquet of yellow he-loves-me-he-loves-me-not daisies exploding in the center of each plate, now scorched and curled around the edges. They were ones she had never used, her wedding present from Sonny. She had given him a fine leather briefcase with his initials stamped in eighteen-carat gold. If she could get the briefcase back, she would change the initials to S.O.B.

"This's it," said Tony, gesturing into the room.

"I didn't think it would be so bad."

"I told you."

"I know, but I couldn't picture it," Liz said, shaking her head.

If Tony had been sitting at the kitchen table, she thought, eating his boiled potatoes and tuna fish out of the can when the stove blew, there'd be little parts of Tony all over. They'd still be mopping up. Suddenly she realized she had saved Tony's life by cooking his dinner.

"Come on. In here," Tony called from the living room. Skirting the glass and muddy puddles, Liz picked her way across the kitchen. The shaft of light from Tony's high-beam flashlight played on the dead eye of the picture window before moving slowly across the shelves. The television, tape deck, turntable, and receiver were in their usual places but shriveled like old fruit. Striations climbed the wall behind them like black flames.

When he flashed the beam across the floor, she saw the nylon rug stuck in hard nodules to the woodgrain linoleum. The beam hovered for a moment above the coffee table where a muscle magazine still lay open, then rested on the Danish modern sofa where Tony had kissed her for the first time. The cushions were disheveled, stained, and heavy with water. As her eyes inched across disaster's unruly terrain, she tried to decide which losses were real and which a stroke of good fortune. Some, she thought, surely carried with them the thrill of divestiture as the burden of possession and its concomitant responsibility went up in smoke.

"That's no real loss," she said at last, pointing to the sofa as if Tony could see her finger. He did not answer. The light seemed to float around the dark room of its own accord, illuminating everything except the man who held it. Sometimes it was an act of faith for her to believe Tony was even there.

Without warning the beam shifted sharply and pointed toward the bedroom. Following it, she saw the wall between the bedroom and living room had been broken out. The jagged studs looked like formations in a cave they once toured on vacation in the islands. It was a pirate cave that wound for miles before opening out onto the sea where the cutthroats made their escape. Every time she slipped on the smooth, wet rocks, Tony had caught her under the arms saying, "Steady now."

She expected the bedroom to look like the living room: everything almost the same only altered, like a person with an incurable disease that had been diagnosed but had not yet flowered. "Oh!" she said, as the light revealed the charred Formica chest and headboard, the mattress and springs burned black and pitched up against the wall. The lamps still stood in the centers of the night tables, but the shades were missing and the bulbs broken off in their sockets.

Tony explained how the bedroom and kitchen shared a wall, how the closet backed up against the stove, and how his clothes fueled the fire; but Liz was remembering the cave, its intricate tunnels and a confusion so great that she didn't realize they had doubled back to the starting point. When they came out into the bright afternoon sun, their rented car in plain view, she blinked as though she had entered another country.

"Now do you see?" Tony concluded, flashing the beam into her eyes.

"Yes, but what about the wall?" she asked, pushing the hand that held the light back toward the exposed studs.

"The firemen broke it out."

"But why?"

"To get into the bedroom," said Tony with patient exasperation.

"Why couldn't they use the door like everyone else?"

"Liz, they were rushed," he said, clipping each syllable.

"Then they're idiots," she said. "They think they're hotshots," she continued, swept up in indignation's fast current, raising her voice with each new thought. "Just because they run red lights and blast sirens and everybody jumps they think they can come into a person's house and chop down walls. They probably really get off on it. They probably go home and knock their wives around."

"Think of it this way," said Tony quietly, kicking at one of the studs, "I could've been in here."

An image of Tony as shriveled and black as a woman they once saw displayed in a glass case in a Seattle tourist shop flashed into Liz's mind. A card taped on the wall beside the case said the woman had died a sudden death in the desert a hundred years ago, her body preserved by the dry heat. Liz had looked at the woman's long, leathery breasts and into her mouth at her rotten teeth. It isn't right, she had thought, to suffer an ordeal like that and then turn up as exhibit A. The card identified the woman as Sylvia, a ridiculous name for a woman like her.

"You could've been here, too," said Tony. "We could've been in bed. We could've been making love when it happened."

Liz shuddered. "Let's get out of here."

Back outside she still smelled the smoke's acrid fumes, which, she finally realized, she had carried away in her own hair and clothes.

That night she had trouble falling asleep. She could not capture the put-away-for-the-night and ready-to-start-the-week feeling she usually had. She tried to lull herself to sleep by figuring out just how well she really knew Tony. In her head she multiplied weekends by years to calculate how many times she had slept with Tony. But then she remembered there were variables. Vacations, for example. Seattle, San Diego, Corpus Christi, Miami, Charleston, Boston, destinations that radiated like spokes from the hub of the Midwest, always toward a coast, an edge to step off of. Finally she fell asleep reciting the states and their capitals, beginning in the corner with Washington.

Four weeks later Tony was still sleeping in Liz's bed. When she asked him about his apartment, he said the landlord hadn't even started the repairs. Insurance problems, he told her. Finally she emptied the bottom dresser drawer for his clothes. This meant she had to move the Wedgwood down to the basement storage locker, even though she paused to admire it each week when she cleaned the bedroom.

At 3:00 A.M., even though it was only Friday, Tony reached for her breast for the first time since the fire. A few minutes later she told him not to worry, that it was all psychological and he'd be all right once things got back to normal. "Go back to sleep," she told him. "You can still catch a couple of hours." Tony had to get up at 5:00 to start work at the plant by 6:30. Instantly, it seemed to her, he slept. Thoroughly awake, she flipped on the reading light clipped to the headboard, hearing her own irritation in its annoying click. Tony's eyes flickered open in dull surprise.

"What're you doing?" he asked, his voice sleep soused.

"Can't sleep. I'm going to have to read myself to sleep," she said, reaching for *Hawaii* on the nightstand.

Because she thought new books with their shiny covers and surprises were like strangers breaking into a house, she reread the same books until the characters were familiar as family.

"You can learn about things," she had told Tony, when he pointed out that she had been reading *Hawaii* ever since they had met. "These people do research. Reading *Hawaii* is almost the same as going there."

Nearly every night Liz dreamt of water—deep blue, serene in its slow wash as a tailor unfurling yard after yard of rich azure cloth from an endless bolt. Her dreams followed the coast, moving slowly along its edge as if filmed from a boat in deep water. Beyond the waves, a glittering strip of white sand mediated between the vibrant blue and the neon green palms fringing the beach. The dreams were perfect, unpeopled, so beautiful she hated to wake up.

She rested the book on her stomach and opened it to chapter one where Michener created Hawaii. *Millions upon millions of years ago,* she read, settling quickly into the sentence she knew by heart, *when the continents were already formed and the principal features of the earth had been decided, there existed, then as now, one aspect of the world that dwarfed* ...

"Light's in my eyes," mumbled Tony, stretched out on his back.

"So roll over on your side," she said. *Millions-upon-millions-millions-upon-millions-upon-millions-millions-of-years* ...

"I can't sleep on my side."

In the silence that was her reply, he slept again. When he woke, it was to a sharp pain in his knee. She kicked him again, a slam-bam karate move he had taught her in the self-defense program he had customized for her.

"Yeow!" he yelped, clutching his knee to his chest as if preparing to execute a cannonball off the high board.

"Snoring," she explained, turning the page.

"Huh?"

"You're snoring so loud I can hardly read. Turn over."

"It's my sinuses."

"Turn over," she insisted. She was silent for the few paragraphs it took for the explosions of fiery lava to crash and build layer upon layer until a mass no larger than a man's body finally pushed itself above the sea's surface like a squalling infant entering the world. Without taking her eyes from the page, she eased Tony's pillow out from under his head with her left hand and pushed it under her own pillow so she could prop up.

Liz woke fighting a blanket thrown over her head. For a minute she thought someone had broken into her apartment and she was being taken hostage. Feeling the empty space beside her, she realized Tony had gotten up. When her hand wandered into a wet spot, she thought she understood. Fluffing the comforter, she found it was also wet, along with her nightgown. She sat up and switched on the reading light. When she flung back the covers, the realization that had been taking shape became jarringly complete, like a drifting boat bumping land.

Jumping up, she threw off her gown and began stripping the bed. Comforter, blankets, sheets, mattress pad. She went into the bathroom and stood over Tony. Hunched on the toilet with his head in his hands, he looked small. He looked like a stranger.

At first he did not say anything. "I was having a dream," he finally began because her presence seemed to demand a response, "and then it happened." Although the words were muffled, hearing his voice assured her Tony was still Tony. Partly out of relief, she began to speak emphatically.

"I've had those dreams too. I've had dreams in which I was actually sitting on the toilet, I was actually *going*, for God's sake, but I still woke up and got out of bed. One time just *having* the dream was relief enough. I rolled over and went right back to sleep."

Tony stood up. He was naked from the waist down. The wet edge of his pajama top was stained in a pattern that looked like a row of miniature volcanic peaks. "Liz," he said quietly, gripping her bare arm, "I'm not you."

Pulling away, she went into the bedroom and gathered up the bedding, careful not to touch any of the wet places. "All this stuff has to be washed," she said when she returned, dumping it into the bathtub. It was after 5:30.

"Why don't you just put it in the machine?" Tony asked.

"Not possible. You don't even put a diaper in the machine until you've washed it out. No, you have to wash everything first," she said, her voice ripe with the self-righteous authority that injury sometimes confers.

In the kitchen she scrubbed her hands with a vegetable brush and then scoured the sink. Jabbing the red button that would start up the coffeemaker, she decided not to go to work. She would stay home and read *Hawaii*. She would stay home until she finished it.

Tony pushed up his sleeves and reached for the tap. Stopping short, he slammed it with the heel of his hand. He dragged his pajama top over his head without unbuttoning it, threw it in the tub with the rest of the laundry, and dressed for work. He skipped breakfast and left the sack lunch he had prepared the night before in the refrigerator. Although the food in the cafeteria at the plant was both bad and overpriced, he would rather eat it or even go hungry than return to the kitchen with its thick brew of percolating coffee, cleanser, and recrimination.

When Liz was sure he was gone, she went into the bathroom, grabbed a can of disinfectant from the cabinet under the sink, and sprayed in wild sweeps as if she were combating a swarm of killer bees. Shutting the door, she spent the day on the couch buried under her blue angora afghan with Michener, hoping, like all travelers, to discover a more hospitable clime.

Liz stiffened when she heard Tony's key turn in the lock. At 3:30 sharp, he pushed open the door. The scuff of his heels on the kitchen tile told her he had walked on the Chinese rug without removing his boots. A ripple of anger rose from the base of her spine and climbed her vertebrae like lava racing toward the stony field of her cranium where it would explode. Still she did not move. After several soundless minutes passed, she crept toward the kitchen. Tony sat at the breakfast bar with his back to her. Balanced on the edge of the tall chair, he was busy untying his laces. Bent at the waist, he looked huge, mountainous, and the sudden desire that flamed inside her was couched in terms she had not considered until this moment. She would test the laws of physics: immovable object, irresistible force. Rushing him from behind, she grabbed the back of the chair with both hands, threw her full weight against it, and pushed while twisting sharply to the left. Toppling heavily toward the floor, legs crumpling beneath him, shirttail disengaging, Tony struck his head against the counter's metal rim. When he looked up at her, a red knot was already rising on his right temple.

"I wish you weighed two hundred pounds," he said quietly, showing her his clenched fist.

She knew he would pack his duffel bag, fill it again with the grip exercisers and the weights and the bookends with their busts of Abraham Lincoln, and she knew she wouldn't try to stop him.

When Liz opened the bathroom door, the shrill mix of urine cut with ammonia slashed at her like a hoodlum's bright blade. She flipped on the fan and held her breath while she doused the bedding with bleach. Opening the spigot full blast, she filled the tub to the brim with hot water. As an afterthought she emptied in the rest of the gallon jug, causing a backwash that sloshed over the edge and threatened her furry blue slippers. "High tide," she said aloud, raising her right arm, palm up, like a conductor asking the orchestra for a crescendo. The slammed door banged back on itself, resounding with a loud ta-dum!

In the living room she pulled the afghan up to her chin, flipped open *Hawaii* and set out for Molokai, its airy syllables belying the weight of human misery in the realm of lepers, the fingerless working their wrist spoons, the toeless hobbling on their stumps, the faceless blind behind their veils, the violent marking their prey. Latched in their wicker cage on the *Kilauea*'s rocking deck, the banished were haunted by the cries of their husbands or wives or mothers from whose arms they had been wrenched by law. *"Auwe, auwe!"* they wailed, the long vowels uncurling like hands reaching after the ship launched from Honolulu's clean, white shore.

Although the *Kilauea* had only just sailed, Liz found she could no longer ignore the bedding simmering in its chemical lake. Obligation ate at her like a disease. Leaping from the sofa with an angry burst of energy, she grabbed a sturdy wooden yardstick from the hall closet. In the bathroom she poked and churned the thick soup of disaster, glimpsing large white patches where the bleach had robbed the pink sheets and blankets of their color. She thought of certain whales that flashed their barnacle-dappled backs when they surfaced and rolled before disappearing into deep water. Draining the tub, she wrung the sopping linens until her hands were numb from the bleach. When she flicked her thumb across the tips of her fingers, she felt nothing.

Gathering up the first heavy still-dripping load in her arms, she carried it through the hall, across the pale blue Chinese rug, and down to the basement laundry room. The wet ends of the sheets slapped against her thighs and then snaked around her calves, hobbling her.

Back in her apartment she set the timer to ring five minutes before the load would finish. Sometimes other tenants cut in if the machine had stopped. Sitting down at the breakfast bar in Tony's empty chair, she opened her book to check on the progress of the lepers. While she read, with her thumbs and forefingers she absently sectioned off two wiry curls over her forehead and twisted the hair into tight little springs. Then she moved down to her temples.

When the timer sounded she carried the second load to the basement, *Hawaii* tucked under her arm. After one cycle in the tiny windowless room, the humidity was high enough to send rivulets coursing down the gray walls. Most of the floor tiles were loose, and mold blossomed on the concrete floor where others were missing. Overhead the long fluorescent tubes flickered violently. She dumped the sodden blankets on top of the dryer and opened *Hawaii* on top of them. Mun Ki and Nyuk Tsin, husband and wife, leper and his *kokua*, were about to attack Big Saul, the leper tyrant, with sticks sharpened to wicked points. Eyes racing across the page, Liz took up the two remaining clumps of hair at her nape and twisted them until her scalp stung. Noseless, his fingerless hands as big as hams, Big Saul was still a powerful man who greeted all those who were flung into the sea from the *Kilauea*'s heaving deck, the ship unable to land on the lazaretto's rocky promontories. *Here there is no law*, he thundered. *There is nothing but what I command.*

One stick entered through his ear and the other tore up through his belly. Lurching from the lean-to he had entered with rape on his mind, he clutched his wounds like Polyphemus, the one-eyed giant who staggered under Odysseus' hand. Now order would slowly come to the Lonely Isle. A school, a hospital, a garden.

Before the first row of taro had been planted, Liz felt the heavy air close in on her. It pressed against the full length of her body like a wet sheet. She inhaled deeply, but could not catch her breath. When she inhaled again, a sharp pain navigated her midriff. She leaned on the dryer with both elbows and held her head in her hands. The pain ricocheted from one side of her rib cage to the other like a miniature lightning bolt. *Gas,* Tony would have told her. *I could be giving birth and he would call it gas*, she mumbled. She began to pant like a woman in labor she had seen in a movie, slowly at first, then rapidly. So this was what it would be like to have Tony's baby. For a moment she imagined herself dressing Tony's son in a frilly pink outfit, a lacy bonnet framing his mean, dark, little face. Between pants, she cursed first Tony and then the baby.

When the pain subsided she straightened up. Picking up *Hawaii* and flipping the pages at random, Big Saul again bellowed, *Here there is no law!* Her eyes wandered from the white page onto the washer's shiny, blank surface that her face slid right off of when she opened the lid after the machine chugged to a stop. She looked inside as if she expected the answer to some unspoken question to take shape before her eyes. St. Agnes offering advice about bodily purity, Father Damien sailing in from Belgium, or the Lady of the Lake, maybe, magical, vaporous, rising from the depths waving a scroll that would tell Liz what to do next.

From the maze of twisted sheets a series of sharp odors assailed her like arrows. One by one she pulled the sheets and pillowcases out of the washer and dropped them onto the bacteria-rich tiles. When she slammed down the lid, again her reflection leapt into view. Little spikes of hair stuck out around her head like a thorny crown. Under the flickering fluorescent tubes she looked frantic, even though she was standing still.

The Hard Fact

FELICIA'S ARM STILL HURT WHERE HER MOTHER HAD struck her when she came home after school. At fifteen she was too old to be hit Maggie had admitted when she apologized to her daughter right before bed.

That night Felicia had to sleep with her mother since they were moving the next morning and her own bed had already been stripped and dismantled. Felicia lay down with her back to Maggie and waited with her eyes open while her mother on the edge of the bed rubbed lotion on her arms and legs and vaselined her lips, elbows, and knees.

"Go to sleep," Felicia said at last. "I never stay up this late unless it's an overnight."

"So think of it as an overnight," her mother said.

"I wouldn't have an overnight with someone who slapped me."

"So," Maggie said, "think of it as an overnight with a mean friend." She laughed, falling back on the bed against Felicia who pushed her, but only a little bit so it could be construed as accidental. Then Maggie was up and tickling her all over the way Maggie's own father had sometimes tickled her when she was a little girl and balked at rising for mass. She tickled her daughter's ribs and under her arms. She gripped Felicia's left foot between her knees like a blacksmith shoeing a horse and tickled the sole, but Felicia got free after one good kick because Maggie was so slippery. When Maggie wrestled her down again, she wiggled her daughter's toes and began reciting "This little piggy" until Felicia gave in as Maggie knew she had wanted to all along. Together they laughed until the nearly empty bedroom echoed. Felicia understood this was her mother's way of apologizing.

The move would be a small one. It was less than a mile from the fifth floor apartment where Maggie and Felicia had lived for thirteen years to the brick bungalow where, in Felicia's words, they would live like a real family. Felicia would attend the same school, and Maggie would shop at the same grocery and cash her alimony checks at the same bank. But they would live close to the ground. When they looked out the windows they would see the dependable trunks of oak trees instead of empty sky.

The last night in their apartment neither mother nor daughter thought about the empty house waiting to receive them, and they didn't think about their argument. That night Felicia's friend had been on the late news. He was in her class but stood a head shorter than she. Dark, small-boned, frail looking, he had hid behind his aunt who shielded him from the camera while the voice-over told how his mother had killed his father, and then herself.

Robert, Felicia's father, had tried to use his daughter as a weapon against Maggie during their divorce. At first it was smart politics, and then it became habit. He had filed for custody of the toddler, confusing parenthood with ownership, love with obsession, desire with revenge. During Felicia's visits with Robert, he described her future in his household: a doll with blonde hair, twin to herself; a puppy that would come to whatever name she gave it; a shaggy pony that would eat apples from her hand. As he spoke he imagined himself gesturing grandly toward the row of pet store cages and his daughter's breathy gratitude when he wrote out the check. By the following day he had forgotten that scene and was constructing another, no less real to him. Felicia was not yet five when she came to understand the concept of a broken promise.

After the divorce was final, Robert moved across the state line putting four hours by car between him and his daughter. His visits grew infrequent even though he was often in town to check on his dry cleaning business. Every three or four months he showed up unannounced to take Felicia to the carnival or the Ice Capades. In this way he tempted her, and then he withdrew. When she tried to picture her father, he wavered on the perimeter of her imagination like a funhouse spook. With anger and longing she watched him materialize and then fade.

A few days before Felicia turned ten, Robert picked her up for a weekend at his house. He arrived long after the appointed hour saying he'd had an important meeting and complaining how difficult it was to manage his business long distance. Felicia had been sitting on her overnight bag watching television when the buzzer rang. Robert always punched out a little tune that sounded like shave-and-a-haircut-two-bits so she would know it was he. "Coming," she called through the intercom, giving Maggie a quick kiss.

For two hours Robert told his daughter stories about dry cleaning before stopping at a motel. He said he was too tired to drive anymore and that they would continue in the morning. Robert bought a pair of paper swim trunks at the motel shop, and then they put Felicia's things in their room.

The pool was housed under a large glass dome that kept the air warm and moist as a greenhouse. Because of the hour, they had the pool to themselves. "The last one in is a pickled pig," Robert yelled, flinging himself into the water. Back and forth they swam, racing each other with crazy handicaps Robert invented. Once it was the Australian crawl, but they had to wave at each other each time they took a breath. Felicia's favorite was a kind of breaststroke they did on their backs but with one knee bent so it stuck out of the water. Those were humps on Nessie's back, Robert told his daughter.

Later they pretended they were trained dolphins and performed a series of dives that carried them the width of the shallow end. Then Felicia stood on her father's shoulders while he duck-walked along the bottom, one hand supporting each of her ankles. Without warning he'd rise up and catapult her toward the deep end. To her it felt like flying.

Back in the room, Robert told Felicia she could shower first. She stripped off her wet suit in front of the big mirror, pausing to study her body. Her breasts were beginning to bud and there was a slight shadow on her pubis. Slowly she turned from side to side and then looked back at herself over her shoulder as if posing for a photographer. That's when she saw Robert in the mirror. He was lying on the bed across the room, and through the door she had left ajar he had been watching her reflection. Seeing confusion spread across her face, Robert said, "You're getting a little too big to leave the door open like that." Felicia never knew how long he had watched or if he would have declared his presence had she not seen him in the mirror, and she never told Maggie about the incident because she had buried it too deeply to retrieve.

A year later, on her eleventh birthday, Felicia received a card from Robert. All the available space was filled with his tight script. "Dear Felicia," he began, "Don't believe everything your mother tells you." The litany continued, often circling back to revive an old complaint before concluding, "Someday you'll appreciate the sacrifices I've made for you." He signed it "Sincerely, Dad and Fanny," as if it were the letter it started out to be when he first picked up his pen. Eventually it became clear that Fanny was Robert's fourth wife. Felicia's reply was a silence she had not yet broken.

It took Robert years to learn Maggie was out of his reach, and he never admitted he had lost Felicia as well. She was her mother's daughter with her bedroom eyes, quick temper, and mistrust of men, he concluded, blaming his ex-wife for turning Felicia against him.

So Maggie raised her daughter alone. Once a man had been interested in Maggie, but while he talked to her in the living room, Felicia, then four, dragged his coat from the hall closet and dumped it at his feet. Maggie admired how Felicia had stood in front of the man, so determined, so sure in her convictions, her knees so sturdy. How high the hanger must have seemed to Felicia, Maggie thought, how heavy the fur-collared coat. She sank to her knees and embraced her daughter, both of them as grateful as if they had been pulled back from the edge of a great precipice. They forgot all about the man on the sofa who had been fervently reciting the one Shakespearean sonnet he knew by heart.

When Maggie slapped Felicia, she was dead tired. She had spent the day packing. At first she enjoyed sorting through the old clothes, books, and photographs, pausing to reconstruct their contexts. Then she was struck by how much of Robert still survived. There was a copy of *Gone with the Wind* inscribed "To my favorite wife" (Maggie had been his second) and photographs of Robert hooking a big fish and straddling the Harley he had bought after he turned thirty. There was the white lace wedding gown, the veil still attached to a sweet beaded cap, and the white guest register filled with names Maggie could no longer match with the faces that crowded the pews of the Gothic church where she had taken one wrong step after another until she reached Robert waiting at the altar. Just finding this evidence made him a fact all over again.

She paused to take a hard look at the past. She considered the difference between the Robert she had married and the Robert she had divorced. In short, he had adored her. Every night when he emptied his pockets he asked if she had gas in her car, money in her purse. To Maggie who was barely twenty, Robert, ten years her senior, seemed paternal, wise. She felt watched over. Archangel Bob, she had called him.

She couldn't remember exactly when he had started phoning her from work. If she didn't answer, at dinner he'd say, "I called at noon, but you weren't here. And then I called at three." He began stopping by the house at odd hours during the day on the pretense he had forgotten a key he needed or a telephone number, ascribing, Maggie eventually learned, his own infidelities to her. This continued even through her pregnancy and Felicia's infancy. The archangel shrank to a mosquito Maggie wanted to swat and then to something vague, like an itch. Maybe Robert had stayed the same, Maggie concluded, and she had simply grown up.

After loading everything into her collapsible wire grocery cart, she wheeled it down the hall to the garbage chute. She listened while the story of her life with Robert dropped five floors into the Dumpster below.

In Felicia's room, she began sorting all over again. She found stacks of postcards from Robert dating back ten years. He'd printed simple messages in big letters: WE ARE HAVING A GREAT TIME IN FLORIDA. TODAY I CAUGHT A BIG FISH. and IT IS VERY HOT IN MEXICO. TODAY I SAW A COCK FIGHT. and SPAIN IS PRETTY. THE BULLS ARE VERY BIG. Maggie had not known Felicia had saved these, but there they were, green rubber bands separating the years. She tossed them in the wastebasket along with a clipboard advertising Robert's dry cleaning business. There were also business cards and little pads of notepaper with COME CLEAN printed across the top.

The argument had started as soon as Felicia came home from school. "Look," said Maggie, "it's junk. We can't afford to pay movers to move junk."

"It's my junk. You had no right to take it. I don't go through your things. I don't decide what you should keep or what you should throw away," Felicia said angrily.

"Let's just keep straight who's the child and who's the parent here."

"Yeah. But you're not the only parent I have."

Maggie's arm shot out automatically. A welt in the shape of her hand rose like a birthmark on Felicia's bare arm.

Maggie had hired the new house painted before they moved in. She thought of it as a clean slate, like the soul after confession. As "coming clean," she would have said if she were still married to Robert. There would be no pictures of bad times stamped on the immaculate surfaces.

The first week was a flurry of what to put where, of shopping for new white blinds to hang at the windows and white plates bearing no visible sign of use to stack in the cupboards. Maggie kept Felicia home from school to help. Together they made all of the choices that changed someone else's house into their own. Then they turned back to the daily lives they had put aside.

Felicia returned to school the same day as Mark, the boy to whom the terrible thing had happened. That afternoon she told Maggie he had looked almost the same, like a plate that was not actually cracked but bore a network of tiny veins in the glaze. She thought it was awful how kids who had never especially liked Mark pretended they had always been his friends. They pandered for inclusion, Maggie knew Felicia meant, in the special sorrow that hovered over him. "Isn't it queer," Felicia continued, "how Mark's father is dead and mine is still alive."

"Now, now," said Maggie, who had never confessed to her daughter how many times she had wished Robert dead. Not murder, of course, but a fish bone stuck in his throat or his Impala drifting over the yellow line. She still believed that if she projected these images often enough and with enough intensity Robert would begin to receive them, imperceptibly at first, but finally with the conviction they were his destiny. Mark's mother had been more direct with the husband who had cheated on her. Maggie had to admire that.

Every day Felicia walked to and from school with Mark. Her other friends walked the old route, but he had moved in with his unmarried aunt who lived only two blocks from Maggie and Felicia's new house. Felicia worried about Mark. He had begun to talk about his father. He said he hated his father for leaving the family, that his father was a deserter and a pimp, and that the woman he lived with was a whore. "That's what I told him," said Mark. "I told him 'Don't call me anymore.' He kept talking, so I said, 'Fuck you,' and then I hung up." That was the day before it happened.

Felicia wanted to say she understood, but it wasn't really the same because her father was still waking up each morning, driving to work, and driving home to his new family. Shifting her book bag to her other shoulder, she touched Mark's arm. When she felt him lean into her, she put her arm around his thin shoulders. "I'm sorry," she said at last, trying not to cry for Mark, for Mark's father, for Mark's mother, for her father, for her mother, and for herself. Then she pulled him closer and rested her ear on the top of his head, as if in this attitude she could receive his thoughts. Her blonde hair fell across his shoulders like a mantle. They walked like that, down the heavily trafficked street toward home. A passerby might wonder how they moved forward when every gesture pulled them sideways into each other.

Felicia didn't tell Maggie everything, even though Maggie thought she did. Her talks with Mark made her feel older, more complete, more herself and less her mother's daughter. So when Maggie asked, "Does Mark talk about it?" she said, "No. No one talks about it. Everyone pretends it didn't happen."

If Mark ever went back to his old house, he would see what Felicia saw when the new owners asked her to baby-sit for their young son. They said she came highly recommended and that they would pick her up at nine on Saturday morning. They would be gone for the day. Felicia didn't recognize the address over the telephone, but she recognized the house when they pulled into the driveway. It looked the same as it had on television the night she and Maggie suddenly stopped arguing.

While the boy played in the backyard, Felicia watched him from the kitchen window. He kept looking up to make certain she was still there. She smiled and waved to reassure him, but she couldn't stop remembering the story she had pieced together from the news, school gossip, and Mark's confessions about the Saturday that had ruined his life. When she heard the mailman on the front porch at eleven, the hour Mark's father had visited his own house at the request of his estranged wife, she saw the mother open the door for the father who shielded himself with bravado of the sort Robert used when he knew he was in the wrong. He came as a trespasser from the bed of the woman Mark had called whore. The mother, wearing a new flowered dress bought with the father's money, invited him in and shut the door behind him.

Felicia moved the father and the mother through the script like the tiny figures with pliable arms and legs that had lived in her dollhouse when she was a child. Because she had not known Mark's parents, his mother took on the face of Felicia's mother when she spoke the first accusation; his father took on the face of Felicia's father when he retaliated. The mother went upstairs. Then she came down with one hand behind her back. When the father opened his mouth again, the bravado was gone. His thoughts banged against each other like cars on a downhill freight. From among them he had to choose the one that would stop this tragedy and return him to the safe plateau he thought he had been standing on all along.

The first shot went through his left palm, which might have been raised in a gesture that made him look like a cop directing traffic. This, Felicia knew, had occurred in the kitchen where she now listened to the refrigerator start up and shut down with a shudder. She reached out and touched the door Mark's father had opened in a happier time to hunt for a can of beer or the leftover meatloaf wrapped in aluminum foil he would share with his son while they watched the baseball game on TV.

Holding his hand as if it were a stranger's just met, the father left the kitchen and made his way toward the staircase. Felicia followed him up the steps he climbed like a child, bringing his right foot up beside the left and standing on a single stair before advancing, in this way doubling the length of the journey. Outside, the little boy called, "Felicia! Felicia! Come here!" Maybe he had hurt himself, maybe he wanted to play, but Felicia pushed his cries to a place where they mingled with the cries of the father and the mother. The cries were short, intermittent, like spatters on a freshly painted wall.

The second shot tore into a place the father could not see or cradle like his hand. Still he climbed, weighted by the lead in his back, heavier than any scale would show a bullet to weigh. Felicia stared at the wall at the top of the stairs where he had leaned. She imagined it yielding to his body; she imagined two barely perceptible indentations, one for his shoulder, one for his hip.

For the father, the telephone just inside the master bedroom had become an object of desire that rivaled any he had ever felt. He hunched his shoulder as if he were holding a receiver against his ear. Picturing the small numbered squares give way beneath the fingers of his good hand, he followed the call out of the house along wires lined with birds still as tin cutouts in a shooting gallery shut down for the night. Then, because there was nothing else to do, he planned how he would say *My wife has killed me.*

The new owners didn't have an upstairs phone, but the little plastic jack that had meant everything to the father was screwed into the baseboard near the door. Beside it stood the mother, her anger spent but harboring in its place the resignation her husband had felt when the first bullet took his hand. Now the little boy was blubbering *Fe-li-cia-Fe-li-cia-Fe-li-cia* over and over like an underground spring. She looked through the window of the ordinary room to see what the mother had seen: the lilac bush laden with blooms, the small plot planted with tomatoes and sweet peppers, the bare patch under the swing the father had hung from the limb of the oak tree, the boy kneeling in the dirt. But on that other day the lilac was not yet in flower and if the mother had seen a little boy, he was a memory of a younger Mark.

Felicia hurried to finish the story of the mother who bore the face of her mother, the mother who bore her own face, the trigger-happy mother who somewhere in this room had spoken her last words to the dead husband who would be buried beside her after she held the barrel of the .32 Magnum, illegally bought and owned, against her chest, the barrel round as a coin that she would use to buy her passage out of this tragedy. To leave the bedroom, Felicia had to pass the father who lay by the door. He stared up at her with eyes as blank as Robert's the night he had watched her in the mirror. She took one giant step over the body, and then it was behind her.

By the time Felicia reached the little boy, his eyes were red and swollen, his shirt strung with loops of drool. Pulling him close, she cried until he began to comfort her in the way that children do. When the new owners called Felicia the following week, Maggie heard her say that her mother no longer permitted her to baby-sit.

In the kitchen, Maggie was fixing vegetarian spaghetti sauce, a triple batch so there would be leftovers to freeze. She believed it was time to have a serious talk with her daughter about death, a talk like the ones they'd already had about not getting into cars with strangers, menstruation, and the moral defects of teen-age boys. She called Felicia to cut up the tomatoes and peppers.

"Sometimes death takes us by surprise," Maggie began, clamping the opener onto a can of tomato paste. "It's something the living are left to work out."

"Do we have to talk about this now?" Felicia asked.

"Talking demythicizes it."

"What?"

"I mean if we talk about it, it gets littler instead of bigger. I've had experience. Listen to me and you'll be ahead of those girls who don't talk to their mothers." Maggie turned the handle briskly, sending the sharp little wheel on its track around the tin lid. "Look," she continued, "I've known people who died."

"Like who?"

"My grandmother died. And my grandfather."

"That's different. They were old."

"Okay. It's different. But it's loss all the same."

Each time Felicia cut open an overripe tomato from the backyard garden, it splattered seeds and juice across the white countertop. She worked slowly, pushing the seeds around with the tip of the knife to make shapes she changed into something else whenever Maggie glanced in her direction.

"When I was in high school I knew a girl who died. She was popular. The prom queen," Maggie said, taking the knife from Felicia and wiping off the counter.

Because Felicia looked interested, Maggie hurried out the details of the gas leak, the asphyxiation, and how the pretty girl in the robe and crown at the coronation became a photograph in a yearbook with *In Memoriam* written under it in fancy script.

"The whole school went to the funeral. All the girls were crying, and when we filed past the coffin each of us took off a bracelet or ring, something, and put it into the casket."

"What did you put in?"

"I really didn't know her that well."

Felicia dumped the vegetables into the oversized white enamel pot and Maggie stirred them into the thick liquid already simmering on the stove. She mashed the sliced tomatoes against the side with a slotted spoon so the pulp spurted through.

"But it's still not the same," said Felicia. "That was an accident."

"And the shooting was an accident, too, but of a different sort," Maggie concluded, wanting to prove a point.

Felicia turned suddenly and left the kitchen. She didn't answer when Maggie called after her, "Felicia, come back here!" The second time Maggie called, her voice sounded like an echo to Felicia who could hardly hear her mother through the closed bedroom door.

So Maggie didn't tell her the story that began "Once I almost married a man who died." She knew Felicia would be interested when she got to the part about how Felicia hadn't liked him, even though he always brought her a book or little toy. Maggie had thought that Felicia, with her intuition and child's eye, had seen death circling his head like a black halo.

The man and Maggie began dating the summer he turned forty, when Felicia was four. He wrote a poem about how he believed love was possible for him, how it would balance, finally, his cynicism, his despair. Maggie knew all along she was not what he really wanted but rather that she was an intermediary who would lead him past the promise of love to the thing itself.

The cancer must have been growing in his brain while they had argued about Felicia—he didn't want to raise another man's child—and while he recited "Shall I compare thee to a summer's day?" When he reached the line, "Rough winds do shake the darling buds of May," he pursed his thin lips around the words so his mouth looked delicate, temporary, like a miniature rose. He pursed his lips again when he was interrupted before the final couplet he had planned to render with a flourish. When Maggie led him to the door he had insisted, "But how many men can give you Shakespeare off the tops of the their heads?" The question required her to put a man reciting Shakespeare on one side of the scale and little Felicia on the other. She broke off the relationship. And then he died.

Her therapist had told her to write down everything she would say to him if he were still alive, but Maggie couldn't talk to the dead.

She couldn't get past the first sentence with its curious implications: *I slept with a man who died.* So she didn't write about how she had lost her chance to save him, but had instead verified his deeper belief that one person is incapable of loving another, no matter what Shakespeare said.

Through the closed door, Maggie heard "Twist and Shout" playing on Felicia's tape deck. She turned down the flame under the sauce, which had reached a rolling boil. Maybe it didn't matter whether or not Felicia heard the story she would only say was not the same. And how could Maggie even tell her the story she couldn't tell to herself. Besides, she didn't want to talk anymore. She didn't want to think anymore, but she couldn't block the hard fact of her Felicia walking home beside Mark, an arm around his shoulders, her tears spilling over the both of them. She remembered how she drove past them with no sign of acknowledgment, how to them her car was no different from any other on the road, how she drove blindly, missing street after street, with no poem or hopeful prayer on her lips.

Smaller Than Life

LARRY INCHES HIS STOOL CLOSER TO THE BAR IN DAVE'S basement without taking his feet off the rungs. His colleagues at the small, failing college where Larry teaches business English laugh at each small hop as the stool advances. They always laugh when Larry gets drunk, but he is the one who wakes up alone in the mornings and sits all day with his head in his hands.

"Scotch?" Larry says to Dave. Ordinarily Larry would get the drink himself, but he doesn't want to stand up. When Dave goes behind the bar, Larry leans to the left so Dave's body blocks the neon light from the flashing Old Style sign. His head brushes Frieda Markovitz's shoulder. She teaches in Women's Studies and moves out of Larry's reach.

"Head up, Larry. No more mama to lean on," she says, shaking her head over the sad need of grown men everywhere.

"You're a charmer, Frieda, but that spiky shoulder's not for sleeping." Larry smiles, feeling he's scored a point for himself and all men. Frieda rolls her eyes and then studies Dave who she wishes would leave his wife.

Taking off his glasses, Larry places them on the bar in front of him to make them look like they're looking back. He slouches on the stool and puts his chin on the bar so he can look through them.

Everything behind the glasses is smaller than life, even the flashing light, and everything in front of them, including Frieda, is larger with soft edges that waver and merge. This is the true meaning of double vision, thinks Larry. Startled by his profundity, he is suddenly happy.

"Hey Frieda," he jokes, "I'm seeing double. You got two eyes and two tits."

"Watch your language, buddy. That's *you've* got two eyes and two tits," she says, underlining the *you've* with an index finger.

Larry reaches for the capable finger looming above him. He catches it with some difficulty and draws it to his lips. He can't decide whether to bite it or kiss it.

"Honey, you got class," he says," scooping up his glasses, tossing them in a one-handed juggle, and flipping them onto his face. "Want to hear the story of my life?"

The others are in the back room playing Chubby Checker and dancing the Twist. Everyone is wearing a different kind of hat, a tradition at Dave's end-of-the-year parties. Once the party cranks up, they'll start trading the hats: the aviator cap for the Stetson, the mouse ears for the beret with the orchid plume. Larry thinks the hats are dumb. He thinks people wear them to forget who they are, and he hates to dance. It makes the blood pulse in his temples. He imagines the red and white corpuscles as two opposing teams colliding on the field of his brain.

Silver Springs, Florida. 1951. Larry was seven and the family was taking their summer vacation. Mom, pop, Larry, and baby sis. They were floating in a glass-bottom boat with another perfect, all-American family and a bored guide who dropped a ball of dough into the crystal clear water. As it drifted toward the bottom, two schools of fish, one gray and the other blue, darted after it, zigzagging in unison, as if they were passengers in the same car. "Football," the guide declared unconvincingly, but everyone smiled as if this were the Rose Bowl. Even then Larry knew games were more complex, that they eventually arrived at a face-down-on-the-playground-bloody-nosed standoff that put you in or out of the tight circle of peers that meant life or death for the rest of the school year or as long as memory lasted.

Remembering the vacation causes Larry to think about a postcard he's saved in his top dresser drawer since middle school. It shows a smiling woman riding a dolphin and waving at the camera. Even though the woman looks like she's having a good time, Larry always wanted to be the dolphin. What bothered him was the rope tied like a noose around the dolphin's nose. When he first got the card, Larry carried it around for a couple of weeks, and at night he propped it up on the desk beside his bed.

Sometimes he still dreams he is the dolphin. In the childhood dream he'd dive so deep the woman couldn't follow and then, at the very bottom, he'd find a sharp rock sticking up and rub the rope against it until every strand was cut. Larry knew the plan would work because he saw the Lone Ranger get free this way once. Afterward, he would swim to an unmapped sea filled with branching coral and brilliant pulsing flowers where he would live forever. Larry tries to remember who sent the card.

In the back room someone cranks up the volume, and Chubby gets more emphatic. *We're gonna twis-ty twis-ty twis-ty until we tear the house down,* he insists. Larry glances over his shoulder but stays at the bar. The dancers flail and jerk like gerbils on amphetamines, loyal to the music until it grinds out its last *Ee oh Twist*. Frieda stays to watch Dave and Larry watches her. Dave's wife, who has put their two-year-old to bed, now sinks down beside Frieda with a sigh of mock relief. "Back from the wars," she says.

"You know," begins Larry, "the story of my life is a very short story. I'm forty-three and my life's over. I had a life, but now it's over."

"Knock it off," says Dave. "It's the semester that's over. Next year is going to be good for all of us." He looks at his wife conspiratorially and taps a spoon against his glass, four quick clinks.

Only Larry and Frieda look up. "The wife and I have some news," Dave says, smiling broadly. "We've got another one in the oven." He raises his glass and then reaches over the bar and pats his wife's stomach. "Here's to family."

Frieda hitches up the front of her blouse.

"Yeah, let's drink to family," Larry says, holding up his glass for a refill. "Kill the soda," he tells Dave. "Yeah, family. I had a family once. I mean I had a girlfriend, and *she* had a family. A boy from her second marriage. I practically raised the kid while Mona, her name was Mona, went to school." Larry lifts his glass, drinks deeply, and then holds it up at eye level and squints as if to calculate the damage. "'Mona,' I say, when she first shows up in business English, I say, 'Mona, you got great teeth. You'd be a real advertisement in a dentist's office.' So she drops my class and signs up for dental hygiene. Go figure."

Frieda forces her eyes away from Dave's wife's stomach. "So what happened? You still saw her didn't you?" she asks, biting her cuticle.

"I saw her all right. I saw her three nights a week. Mondays, Wednesdays, and Thursdays. I saw her for fifteen minutes before she left for class and for fifteen minutes after she got home. The rest of the time I saw the kid. Mona got a certificate in dental hygiene, and me? I got a family."

"Come on," says Frieda, "you took something away from the relationship."

"Yeah, the scars."

On his first date with Mona, Larry had taken her to a disco. He thought she looked the type. It was summer and Larry had worn his safari jacket with the sleeves rolled up. He'd had a few drinks before he picked her up, but he guided her to the bar anyway. It was long and angular, shaped like a boomerang. The swizzle sticks had little plastic boomerangs on the ends. Each time Larry finished a drink, he slipped the swizzle stick into his left breast pocket. He told himself he was keeping count.

When Larry had three boomerangs in his pocket, he felt like talking. "Let's play a game," he said, turning to Mona. "I'll say a word and you use it in a sentence. Sort of like a Rorschach but with words."

The bass-heavy beat massaged his forearms resting on the polished mahogany bar and chugged through his body like a train.

"Okay," said Mona, "I'm game." She looked puzzled when Larry laughed. Larry wondered if she noticed his dental work, the fine gold and silver fillings that must have glinted in the ball of revolving light.

"Well then, here we go. The first word is *heart*."

"*Carp*?" Mona shouted, cupping her ear against the music.

Larry shook his head. *Heart*, he mouthed, tapping out a short-long rhythm on his chest with two fingers.

"Oh," Mona said, nodding. "*Harrrrt*."

"*Lion*," Larry roared, pocketing his fourth boomerang.

"Hey, Leo. That's my sign," Mona said, flashing her perfect teeth. "You must be psychic."

Larry pushes his glasses up on his nose, stabbing the bridge with his index finger. "Frieda, you want to hear about scars, I'll tell you. I try to be like a father to the kid, right? I tell him we'll go to the rodeo, him and me and Mona. I think he'll like that because of how he always shoots back at the TV."

"Is there shooting at rodeos?" asks Frieda.

"So I pick them up early one Saturday and we drive out to the grounds. The kid is crying because I won't let him sit on my lap and steer. You want to make hamburger out of us, I tell him, and he says Uncle Bob always let him steer. Mona doesn't say anything. She's got a finger in her mouth doing something, maybe massaging her gums. But we get there. We park and start climbing up the bleachers because the kid wants to sit on the top. I'm helping Mona since she's wearing spike heels, and the kid is tagging along behind. Then I feel a sharp sting. I yell and bolt a couple of steps." Larry lifts his glass and swallows before saying in a slow voice, "Now let me ask you, Frieda, what happened?"

"A bee, maybe? A wasp?" Frieda looks helplessly at Dave, but he's got his eyes glued on his wife as if he can see the fetus inside her, curled like a shrimp.

"No one ever guesses," says Larry, shaking his head. "The kid's run up behind me and, get this, bit me in the ass. Rabies, I'm thinking. I grab the little bastard, but Mona's screaming and the kid's kicking my shins. What can I do? I leave them there. That's what a family is for."

At first Frieda can't think of anything to say. "How did they get home?" she finally asks. Her blouse has slipped down again, and Larry watches her breasts move in and out as she breathes. Turning toward her, he feels a hand reaching up through his body, straining toward his heart. He sets down his glass and moves his right hand toward the hand inside him. When he lays it across his chest, he remembers reciting the Pledge of Allegiance in grade school; facing the flag in the corner of the bright room, his voice joins the clear, young voices of the others.

The music stops and the others jostle their way toward the bar, exaggerating their thirst. They are flushed and exhilarated, as though they have just completed a difficult project of great worth.

The fluttering Larry feels is like a distraught hand waving behind a closed window. When he tries to wave back, his head falls toward the bar. The others laugh. "Larry's at it again," someone says. Larry's glasses slip off and begin their silent descent, but he doesn't move to catch them. When they hit, the shattered lenses look like Fourth of July firecrackers exploding in a happier summer.

A History of Swimming

IN THE WOMEN'S LOCKER ROOM AT THE GROVE STREET YMCA, Carla unfastens the twenty-six Velcro tabs on her corset. Because she expects her sprained back to collapse without this support, she hurries to reach the pool and temporary weightlessness.

The walls in the huge room are alive with underwater scenes played out in millions of intricate mosaic tiles. Streamers of seaweed reach toward the ceiling and multi-colored fish browse among them. Starfish and twisty eels linger near the floor, turning the room into a giant aquarium or small reef. Carla, who swims against her will, sees herself as a captive fish, a swordtail, perhaps, in her bright orange tank suit, but a female without the fancy fin.

Descending the ladder into the lane marked SLOW, Carla launches a stroke she has invented, a kind of breaststroke executed on her back. She pushes off, swings both arms out of the water and over her head like oars, and paddles herself from one end to the other. With each frog kick her white knees break the surface like water-smoothed stones. It is the kind of stroke her husband, if she had a husband, would think up an endearing name for.

Earplugs, nose clip, goggles, and a tight cap insulate Carla from the other swimmers. She contemplates the banner suspended from the ceiling at the twenty-five meter mark. FIT FOR LIFE, it reads. The slogan confirms her physical therapist's notion that swimming will not only strengthen Carla's back but also build her confidence. Carla doesn't believe this.

In high school swimming class, Carla had a teacher who couldn't swim. She asked Carla, who was on the swim team, to demonstrate the strokes to the class. While the other girls huddled along the edge, Carla, alone in the pool, shot through the water with grace and beauty. Glancing up, she saw only their legs like a forest of saplings. How could she have known this memory would survive?

Carla tells herself she swims on her back so she can look at the murals and make up stories about how the little fish are forever safe from the big ones, but only on her back can she get enough air. For discipline she swims the Australian crawl every fifth lap. At first she takes three strokes for each breath, but soon she breathes after every stroke, rolling far over on her side and pausing with one arm out of the water while she sucks air into her lungs. The lifeguard, a teenager with big legs, watches Carla until she turns over on her back again. When she does, a man who looks twice Carla's age passes her. He swims a vigorous crawl and his kick churns up a wake that nearly capsizes Carla. By the time she recovers, he has turned and is passing her again.

Carla used to have a lover who was born in Jamaica. He took her home with him at Christmas every year for seven years. All this happened a long time ago. Then, Carla swam without earplugs, nose clip, goggles, or cap. She swam without a suit. Then, her back was as strong as a man's. When Carla tries to remember the trips, they become one long trip. Sometimes she believes she actually lived in Jamaica, and that is why part of her life is missing.

So she can't say when the middle-aged man with the movie camera filmed her as she slept nude on the white sand beach. She can't say which beach it was. Her lover always sat beside her in his trunks and an oversized straw hat with a red bandana tied around the crown. He did not alert her. When Carla woke, the man was less than twenty meters away. He still held the camera to his eye but ducked into the brush when Carla sat up. When he emerged a few minutes later, he still wore his Hawaiian shirt and safari hat, but he had removed his trunks.

Carla darted into the waves, startling a stingray cruising the shallows. It made a jog in its course to accommodate Carla then continued barely disturbed along the shore. It measured more than a meter from wingtip to wingtip. Carla admired the frilled edges of its foreign shape and envied its ease in the water. Ignoring the camera she knew was trained on her back, Carla tracked the ray. She lifted her feet high and set them down carefully. With each step little volcanoes of sand erupted around her ankles. When the ray turned toward open sea, Carla followed.

Twenty-five meters off shore, Carla stopped to look back. Treading water, she watched the man lower his camera and approach her lover. They talked. Her lover gave the man a spliff from the plastic bag he kept under the blanket. The man gave something back. When the man turned and pointed at Carla, her lover began motioning her back to shore. Carla struck out for deeper water.

Below her, hundreds of starfish dotted the white sand—crimson, pink, deep gold, pale yellow. Carla thought of a movie house in Chicago with a dome like a cathedral. An unseen technician made the lights in the painted sky blink like stars on a dark night. Visible proof, Carla thought. But in the water, she looked down instead of up and the sun beat on her back so hard she felt herself shrinking. When she returned to shore, her lover was sitting on the blanket with his arms around his knees. The bandana was missing from the crown of his hat. The next morning, at great expense, Carla boarded a plane back to Chicago. She never saw her lover again.

Once Carla won a first place medal for backstroke at a swim meet the star of her team was too ill to attend. She swam against only one opponent, a girl from her own team. The girl, her name was Rosie, was overweight but kind. Carla swam even with Rosie, matching stroke against stroke, for two of the twenty-five meter laps. On the third lap she lagged one stroke behind. Sensing Rosie's exhilaration after the final turn, Carla surged ahead and won by half a lap. She had accurately judged Rosie as a swimmer with only one pace and no feel for competition. Standing together in the shallow water waiting for their breath to return, Rosie's round, shocked face revealed all she knew about betrayal.

In the locker room the next week the coach distributed the medals. The girls clustered around her, eager to claim the gold, silver, and bronze discs fitted with coy ribbons and safety pins to affix to their sweatsuits. The coach, the star swimmer's mother, began with the seven-to-nine-year-olds and worked her way up to the teenagers. Carla, secure in the knowledge of her tour de force, waited patiently for her reward. One by one the younger girls drifted away. Finally the coach turned to go. Carla had to stop her and explain she had won. When the coach handed over the medal, Carla could tell the woman thought she was lying.

The clock above the diving board confronts Carla as she swims toward the shallow end. With the hands at 6:00 A.M., Carla thinks of herself as a horizontal in a world of verticals. The high ceiling is all skylights but vaulted like a Gothic cathedral. The sun rising on the tiles sets the fish in motion. Twelve small blue and gold discuses flicker near the ladder. When Carla moves in for the turn, she imagines herself part of the school.

What morning was it that Carla and her lover watched the fishermen haul in their nets? One man sat in a rowboat at the apex of a triangle sealed by the shore, and four others, two on each side, stood in waist-deep water pulling in the nets hand over hand. The great resistance caused Carla to imagine them filled with giant fish fighting for their lives. She waited to see what the men would drag from the sea.

The fishermen worked from waist-deep to knee-deep to ankle-deep water. They stepped clear of the sea. The net, folded in half on the shore, subdued the flapping and twisting fish. Carla felt like an archeologist uncovering a lost city or a grave robber breaking into a tomb. She expected fish like jewels in dazzling combinations of lapis, ruby, jade, and amber delivered at last into human hands.

The men joked among themselves in patois and stopped to roll spliffs. The net looked smaller than when it was stretched across the sea and the catch disproportionate to the work of hauling it ashore. Dark blue clouds rolled across the horizon. When the men finally pulled the net open, the fish looked cut from the same dull cloth. Only a few jumped intermittently, others gasped and worked their gills. The fishermen threw out puffers and porcupinefish, not back into the sea, but into the bushes or onto the beach where sand stuck to their eyeballs and seeped into every orifice. The best they put into a bucket rigged with a scale. These they would sell. Only half of the catch was worthy.

The pool room is as steamy as the tropics. The ceramic fish waver as if underwater. Carla thinks the air is made visible by the chlorine rising from the surface. In the Caribbean the air is thick with reggae and burning cane. Men gather on the black-sand country beaches to smoke ganja and cook fish stew in big pots over open fires. When the old man swims past Carla again, she swallows enough water so the chlorine burns her throat.

The man-who-removed-his-trunks had bushy red hair and sunburned arms and legs. Even from a distance Carla could see his white buttocks stark against so much red as he stood over her lover, propped on one elbow on the blanket. Much later Carla saw the man disappearing down the beach, his camera bag slung from one shoulder and his video camera mounted on the other. *Paparazzo*, thought Carla. Beside him was a woman swathed in a long white gauze robe, its hood pulled forward to cover her face. A red bandana trailed from one hand.

After Carla returned to shore her lover carried her into a stand of mangroves rimming the beach. When he pulled down his trunks and lowered himself on top of her, she felt as if she were swimming in open sea. She couldn't get enough air. Every breath burned her throat. The airborne roots of the mangrove cradled Carla like a baby in a basket.

By now Carla has swum enough laps to take her home had the pool been a river leading to the small apartment where she lives with no interruptions. When her therapist asks how the swimming is progressing, she will tell him about the old man.

Afterward, Carla's lover left her on the beach while he went to drink with friends at the roadside bar, a corrugated tin shanty with a thatched roof. The proprietor was a big woman who kept a machete under the counter and served hundred-proof white rum in cloudy glasses, no ice. The men talked with their mouths next to each other's ears to be heard above the bass from the oversized speakers. When one man laughed, the others understood the joke they couldn't have heard. The woman laughed, too, showing the diamond drilled into her front tooth. But even while she was laughing, she kept one hand under the counter.

Carla stayed alone on the beach that afternoon, collecting shells. She piled them next to her blanket before she fell asleep. When she woke, her greatest prizes, spiny stars and baby tritons, sundials and moon shells, were gone. Her lover returned at dusk to find Carla cold, wet, wrapped in a damp towel, watching the sea suck up the last rays of sun. Drunk, he pulled the towel away and pushed Carla down on the sand. She heard only her own breath and the sea rasping against the shore.

When Carla sees the old man swimming toward her, she shifts into the swift back crawl her body suddenly remembers. She stretches above her head and pulls one arm after the other down through the water, flicking her wrist just before her palm surfaces. She surges ahead of the man who, in his surprise, begins to dog paddle. His head bobs at Carla's feet. She launches a strong flutter kick that sends water up his nose. When he tries to stand, he realizes he is in deep water. Carla sees the lifeguard look up from her magazine and rise from her chair. To Carla, who is swimming for her life, the girl seems to move in slow motion.

Carla plans how she will swim to the deep end, execute the flip turn she had mastered in high school, and start back toward the shallow end before the lifeguard can catch her. Visualizing it, her therapist would have told her, will make it real, will draw her closer to the moment that occurs after the turn, after she pushes off underwater, her arms above her head shaping her body into a torpedo or powerful fish, the ecstatic moment when her body breaks the surface midstroke and rises from the chemical-rich mist strong and healed. Suddenly Carla understands she has underestimated herself all her life.

Approaching the wall, Carla tenses her stomach muscles and jackknifes, swinging her legs over her head to plant her feet against the wall. One foot catches in the gutter and drags her body up to the surface. When she twists to release her foot, a spasm starting in her back shoots down her leg like an electric shock. The segment of the day Carla has been trying not to remember snaps into place.

Negril Beach. Christmas Day, 1975. The second time Carla looked back to shore her lover was not sitting on the blanket nor was the man-who-removed-his-trunks anywhere on the beach. Scanning the mangroves, she saw a bright shirt blown open, fluttering like a parrot's wing. The woman in white stood beside the man, auburn hair free of her hood, robe flung open. The camera braced against the man's shoulder pointed sharply down. Carla followed its angle to the red bandana flashing forward and backward in front of the man where her lover knelt.

When her revolving world rights itself, Carla sees the old man, still sputtering, paddle up beside her. His eyes are bloodshot, red-rimmed.

When he raises his arm to grab the ledge, Carla thinks he means to strike her. Shrinking from him, whatever truth she has been swimming toward recedes like a boat leaving the harbor. It changes from fully rigged vessel, to toy, to speck, to nothing. Carla's fogged goggles wall off the murals with the evasive discuses, the sun-filled skylights, memory, everything except the small moment in which she finds herself and the angry red-faced man and the lifeguard with the expansive thighs, opening and closing her mouth like a beached fish.

Four Characters, Three Small Stories

THREE FRIENDS MEET FOR DINNER AT A ROADHOUSE along a minor highway in the country. It is the kind of place that people pass on their way to somewhere else. The man and the two women will spend only an hour together before they get into their separate cars and drive off to separate destinations. Each is busy with no time to waste. Their lives are full of obligation, but once a year they meet at this roadhouse as friends.

The two women arrive minutes apart. They have the habit of promptness their lives require. Each tells the other she looks well. They order white wine, which arrives in plastic glasses. The man is late but offers no excuses. He is a large man and the women look somehow moored by his presence.

The man drapes his overcoat across the back of the fourth chair and rests his hat on the coat's padded shoulders. A passer-by might mistake this for a party of four. The man orders Scotch and the women order more wine. They all order hamburgers. The man says he will have his rare. The women agree they prefer theirs well done. While they wait for their food, the first woman will tell her story.

The subject is cuisine. They laugh about how that is a foreign word in this roadhouse. The other customers are beefy-looking men and tired women who are not their wives. As for decor, bookshelves are painted on the walls and books are painted on the shelves. Titles are painted on the books, but even from a distance the man and two women doubt the lines and squiggles are the alphabet they know. The man builds a case for cuneiform, but the women argue for failure of the imagination.

The first woman begins her story. *Somewhere in France, I don't remember which province, the favorite dish is a kind of bird. It's a little bird, small as my fist* (she demonstrates with one delicate hand) *and baked whole. Lest the implications escape you, I mean the bird is served intact. Although its head droops to one side, lids still cover its opaque eyes and behind the closed beak sleeps a silent tongue. Its feet are drawn up under the body as if it were nesting.*

The others listen attentively and do not interrupt. They look away only to drink. They drink long and eagerly then replace their glasses on the red and white checked oilcloth that gives this occasion the flavor of a picnic.

The bird is a delicacy, she continues, *and you must eat everything. The legs are thin as matchsticks, not even a mouthful. Of course they have plucked the feathers, but otherwise the bird is the same as when it flew from branch to branch. The bird is not a wren or sparrow. I don't remember what kind of bird it is.*

Neither the man nor the other woman knows the name of the bird, but they like the story and applaud the woman who leans back in her chair satisfied she has told such a good story. They order another round of drinks.

The story took longer to tell than I have implied. There were other details the woman had forgotten and therefore other alternatives to suggest, other analogies that tried to translate the image lodged in her brain.

Half the hour is over before the second woman takes her turn. *This is the story of a fish served in Tokyo where, as you know, presentation is important. At this particular restaurant, an ordinary sushi bar, the Japanese chef is a true artist. The fish he will serve rests in a nest of seaweed, and dry ice concealed beneath it sends up puffs of smoke that represent sea foam. The platter is embellished with thin strips of ginger translucent as flesh. In such a cuisine, everything stands for something else.*

The woman pretends to search under the table with her foot as if to confirm her briefcase is still there. Measuring the pause, she concludes, *The chef presents the fish flayed, pink as a baby, carcass still pulsating. He has, you see, served it live, unarguable proof it is fresh.*

The hamburgers are big and nearly cover the plastic plates. Because the man is ravenous he neglects to applaud the story, but the other woman touches her friend's arm in a gesture of appreciation. Without consulting the women, the man orders another round of drinks the way men sometimes do. They pick up their knives and forks and cut the meat. All of the hamburgers are the same—charred black on the outside and raw inside. The woman who told the story about the bird licks off a drop of wine rolling down the side of her glass. The wine is invisible on her tongue.

When the headlights from a passing truck fix the party in its gaze, I realize I have been deceived about their ages. The sudden light reveals their eyes and mouths are appointed with lines and the skin on their throats has begun to loosen.

The man talks louder than he should. *Those are good stories. I like a story that gives the appearance of truth, but I have been listening carefully and notice clues that suggest invention, embellishments and omissions that betray you.*

He spears a piece of bun with his fork and sops up blood from the meat that has pooled in one corner of the plate before continuing. *On the radio I heard an announcement, a contest for school children. It is my habit to listen to the news channel while I bathe. I fill the tub with water so hot that steam clouds the room. I enter the water slowly, one foot at a time, to encourage my body to accept the near-scalding temperature. If I put one foot in and then withdraw it, the line around my ankle is so sharp it looks drawn. Everything on the news channel is true,* says the man. *When I turn up the volume on the radio, the bathroom is dense with truth. And with steam, as I have said before.*

The two women nod their understanding. The other customers in the roadhouse are also listening. Some have turned their chairs away from their own tables and others have gathered around the table for four.

I move the man's briefcase and umbrella onto the floor and sit beside him. When I am thirsty I drink from his glass, although Scotch is not my drink of choice.

In a strident voice, the man resumes his story. *The announcer says many children have been burned playing with matches, others when their houses or apartments caught fire. But he doesn't mention World War II when children in Yugoslavia, for example, lost their hands salvaging gunpowder from grenades, or Hiroshima, that city of raw flesh. Children eligible to enter this contest must know firsthand the meaning of fire. They must write an essay of five hundred words or less telling what they learned. Such children are still children even though the rules require they be burned beyond recognition.*

Exhausted from the effort his story required, the man reaches for his glass but finds it empty. The women avert their eyes and push away their plates. I call for a vote. As usual, one finger means fact and two fingers mean fiction. The man, his two friends, the beefy-looking customers and their companions, everyone votes on the count of three. This is a formality, however, since no one tallies the votes. There is no winner. Everyone pays for their own meal.

THE ECSTASY OF MAGDA BRUMMEL

*Oh, tourist,
is this how this country is going to answer you
and your immodest demands for a different world...*

ELIZABETH BISHOP
from *Questions of Travel*

I

THEY AGREED TO TRAVEL AS FRIENDS. AND YES, THEY would engage separate rooms, never mind that this arrangement would push the trip over budget—for Harry Bagnovich was on a budget—a result of having agreed so suddenly to go. In the end he would sell his car, a 1953 Cadillac, a classic, at great sacrifice to pay his debts and see his way clear from Palermo to Milan along the route Magda had already planned.

Although the world was large, she had chosen to speak to him of the difficulty of finding a suitable companion, her urgency apparent in the pattern her slender fingers wove in the air, in the way her rings caught the light—the thin gold band on the middle finger of her left hand, and the other above it bearing a row of brilliant sapphires crossed by an *x* of tiny diamonds set in platinum, he guessed. Through the flash and sparkle, he caught and held the words "kindred spirit," "time," "money." When she concluded, "Maybe you are such a person," the bulb in the lamp between the two ladder-back chairs where they sat in Magda's living room flickered and blew.

"It's a sign," she said.

"Yes," he agreed, "but what does it mean?"

For weeks Magda Brummel had been listless. She lingered in her robe at the Chinese writing desk, tapping her house keys against its rose marble top until the surface was crosshatched with tiny nicks. She enumerated her losses: she had loved, but she had not married; she had no child to call to her side; an only child herself, she had been left to her own devices and then, too soon, an accident and both parents dead. Midair the wings had faltered, and the plane shuddered to a stop.

At thirty-three, Magda quit her job. She gave no notice but simply failed to appear, leaving behind the potted shamrock on a desk devoid of photographs or clever trinkets. Her smile, more startled than inviting, caused clients to hurry past, preferring to fend for themselves rather than ask for her help, an arrangement everyone found suitable. Practiced as she was in the art of exclusion, the irony of her position as a receptionist had not been lost on her.

Her small circle said she was fortunate to have options, unsuited, they secretly thought, for the world's barter and trade. She could spend but not earn, take but not give. Whatever the rule, she was the exception. Still they called her a good woman who intended the right thing and held no malice in her heart. That she understood none of this allowed them to remain her friends without bitterness or envy.

She kept her rooms simple, unadorned, not out of principle or necessity, but as a concession to her need for space opening around her as in the great cathedrals that encourage the eye upward, toward God. Surrounded by vacancy, she felt trapped. Travel, she finally decided, although she knew it was not the house that confined her but rather something inside her that struck a low ceiling. She would leave her life behind like a cur at a gate. When she returned, she hoped it would be gone.

Each for their own reasons, Harry Bagnovich and Magda Brummel had enrolled in a night school photography class. They were among the dozen separate but like-minded strangers who retrieved the brochures from their mailboxes and thumbed through the pages to Adult Enhancement. Over coffee or lunch, their fingers idly traveled down the listings, pausing at Beginning Photography, which they checked or circled. At the appointed hour, they drove in their separate cars to the local college where they became a class.

When the instructor asked his students why they had enrolled, Magda said she wanted to develop her eye, meaning that she wanted to train it to see the world as a series of perfect compositions, balanced, ordered, warmly lit. This was true, and easier to explain than her need to record where she had been in order to discover where she was going, or her desire to arrest the years that sped off in different directions like high-speed trains departing from a busy station. The photographs would extract scenes of her choosing, stop them cold, and deliver them into her hands where she could study them one at a time to find what she had missed. But even that was not it exactly. There would be images uncaptured by the ordinary eye, there would be shadows, there would be light from no discernable source coaxed into shape, lured back to walkable ground. Propping one elbow on the desk, Magda rested her chin in her palm, four slender fingers striping her cheek, her rings sparking like miniature falling stars.

Harry answered he had time to kill.

Nearly fifty, his wife run off, his children grown, a government job that did not require his full attention, he needed to turn his life around—find an interest, replace loss with satiety, walk out from under the malaise that followed him like a cloud of sour breath. But this, of course, he did not say.

Time to kill. That was the phrase that turned Magda's head toward the right-handed man in the back row wedged into a left-handed desk, his arms folded on its scratched top. Although his silver hair bore no trace of its original color, his boyish face was unmarked by the bump and scuffle of daily life. It was round as a cherub's, innocent and open, an effect marred only by a mustache that bristled above his full upper lip. Magda thought it wolfish, not perceiving it as an indication of complexity that lay below the surface, the tip of something buried, like a protruding root that wound underground across the yard to an oak on the other side. She believed he was a man whose face registered every emotion as if printed in bold type, and on it she read his eagerness to please, a hopeful conviviality.

Shifting in her seat, Magda felt him take in the thin luminous thread of her interest that traveled toward him and send back an unmistakable confirmation. Thread like a vein feeding the heart, thread like a road mapping a destination, and the outline of Sicily materialized in the air—an elongated heart lying on its side, stretched by centuries of accommodation. A circle of tiny lights blinked on, counterclockwise around the perimeter. Such a route would reverse time, she thought, turn back the months and hours, sweep away the present and return her to a happier past. She watched the lights arc north, dotting the mainland. They stopped at the far border where long-fingered lakes branched from the land's open palm. Then she knew she would travel, and she would not go alone.

After the first class, Harry put Magda's face on the woman he nightly conjured to see him through his insomnia. He called up her hazel eyes and marveled at the genetic quirk that had colored half of the right one an arresting blue transfixing him as surely as the arrows that pinned St. Sebastian to the martyring tree. Hazel after the tree, sending down its roots, he thought, sandy loam, or mapped continents, and blue for dusky skies or certain moon-washed clouds. She was a woman, he concluded, in whose eyes heaven and earth resided. When she asked him after class if he were a traveler, he answered the only way he could.

II

THEY HAD BARELY ARRIVED IN PALERMO WHEN HARRY became as aware of Magda as if her every gesture were outlined in light. Her fingertip burned through the map he held open on his palm as she traced the road he had suggested, although her touch was so artful a wren would flourish under it.

The trattoria that first evening opened onto the sea. Ceiling fans turned slowly overhead, lifting the edges of the white tablecloths. With its black and white checkerboard floor and red wrought-iron tables, Harry said they could be in small-town America, the Midwest, circa 1950.

"Except for the sea," she replied, but she knew what he meant. They ordered strips of salmon and artichokes dipped from a rich olive oil bath and tucked into crusty rolls, and beer in quart bottles that encouraged one drink to lead to another. They joked about the American music on the jukebox and, at the same time, marveled how one day of travel could carry them so far from their ordinary lives.

When the trattoria was nearly deserted, Magda leaned across the table and sang along with Aretha Franklin who was spelling out the politics of love. Harry was surprised she knew the words, for he saw her as untouched by the world around her, her reserve a sign of immunity to the passing decades. In spite of that, he had intuited within the Magda he knew only as classmate another Magda with whom he could drink and break bread, one who could lean across the table as she did now and sing.

Harry had been eager to leave the trattoria, to walk beside Magda along this moonlit shore marking the city's heart where, he believed, she again could be tempted across formality's border.

He noticed the black Alfa Romeo the second time it passed. Cruising slowly, it seemed to him ominous, like a flagless ship in open sea.

The third time it passed he called it to Magda's attention, but she merely glanced at the driver he strained to see. The man's olive complexion made it difficult for Harry to discern his features or even the shock of black hair that hung low on his forehead. As the driver passed, he leaned across the passenger seat and gestured at Harry in a way that intimated he should understand. Thief, junkie, Harry thought, although he knew it was Magda who interested the man, the chameleon Magda who became a woman just-met every time Harry's eyes sought hers.

When he mentioned the car again, he watched sobriety fall like a veil across her face. Travelers in a foreign land sometimes imagine harm will step aside for them, preferring instead to strike them down on familiar ground. Magda and Harry were not such travelers.

Hand in hand they ran, ducking into passageways barely wide enough for one, hurrying past dark-shuttered doors that rose right off the cobblestones without the consoling interlude of sidewalk or lawn. Sickly cats slunk into the shadows at the sound of their approach, and both Harry and Magda wished they were able to disappear like that. Harry made abrupt turns, one after the other, until Magda quit counting. They had been lured like rats into a maze, and now they would spend their lives plotting their escape. She had barely formulated this conclusion when Harry stopped. In the distance they heard a car idle for a few moments and then speed away. At the next corner Piazza Pretoria opened in front of them like a clearing. Although she thought they were lost, he had known where they were all along.

When he turned to her in the spirit of camaraderie known to those who have survived peril together, she put her camera to her eye and, leaning against the stone wall of Santa Caterina to steady herself, photographed the Piazza's great fountain. Switching to a telephoto lens, she shot close-ups of the voluptuous bodies of gods ringing the basin, women with modest hands at their crotches, lop-eared oxen with rings in their noses, profiles of noble horses who stared back with vacant stone eyes. The shattered fingers and missing toes would go unnoticed in her developed slides, overshadowed by the luminous white figures asserting themselves against night's backdrop. Like descended angels they had watched over her and guided her back to this place unharmed.

Finally Harry, too, put his camera to his eye. She did not look at him but imagined how he framed his shots, how they must replicate her own, taught, as they had been, to see the same way.

Slowly they walked back to their hotel, passing buildings that still bore, after half a century, scars of the bombing.

Harry was late. Magda paid her hotel bill and sat on a floral sofa in the lobby to wait. In her black linen skirt and black blouse, she looked like a shadow cast across a garden of overblown peonies.

She did not notice the stranger until he stood directly in front of her. Her gaze fell first on his black loafers, traveled up past his too-frankly-present, almond-shaped eyes, then paused at the shock of black hair that fell across his forehead and directed her gaze back down to the hand he had extended. Without asking her name, he explained he had overheard her in conversation and had admired her English. Would she mind speaking with him, he wanted to know, as he had little opportunity to practice the language. Moving his hand to her back, he guided her to the deserted bar off the lobby and ordered for them both from a waiter who treated him with deference.

Magda thought of Harry who by now must be sitting on the floral sofa where she had sat, methodically pulling each finger to crack his knuckles, a nervous habit. She would make him wait only as long as she had been made to wait before she introduced him to this stranger, explaining as he had explained to her that he was a ship buyer from Hong Kong, waiting for a dry-docked vessel to be repaired. He had been in Palermo for three weeks, and still there was no visible sign of progress.

Leaning into her, he kept his eyes on her face but in a way that evaded direct engagement. "You are a traveler," he said in a low voice, "a woman in search of adventure." He spoke in a monotone, as if reading from a script, like the fortuneteller, a palmist, Magda had once visited who guaranteed expertise in finding all lost things. For a moment she was amused. He was a phony, a charlatan, just like the palmist, but something familiar in his manner encouraged her to stay. "You are lonely," he continued, "although you do not travel alone."

Magda rose abruptly, feeling as violated as if she had discovered a spy with his eye to the keyhole. She put her hand on his shoulder to hold him in place. Here was a man no one could trust, a blot on the day, a slippery fish, perhaps with underworld connections, maybe deranged, but what he said held some measure of truth, just enough to hint at credibility, again like the palmist who had found nothing.

When he opened his wallet to pay his bill, Harry saw at a glance his credit cards were missing. The tight fist of panic clenched down hard in his stomach, and acid from his strong breakfast cappuccino traveled up into his throat. He scanned the lobby for Magda but his eyes leapt haphazardly around the large room and he knew he skipped right over the one familiar face among strangers. Made to understand he was causing a delay and must give up his place in line, he sat down heavily in an overstuffed chair and put one hand on each of its upholstered arms like a prisoner awaiting electrocution.

Motionless except for the rapid rise and fall of his chest, he repeated under his breath, *Rich man, poor man, beggar man, thief*. Although it was a senseless litany returned from childhood, its predictability consoled him. Each repetition led him back to the word *thief*. Someone was guilty.

Gradually he became aware of Magda kneeling in front of him. She materialized in slow increments like the Virgin on the hill at Fatima. In his hour of need she had appeared, a favor granted. He did not notice the slight flush along her cheeks, which he might have recognized from the previous night after they eluded the black Alfa Romeo, the only sign she, too, had been frightened.

"My heart," he told her, describing his loss. She asked him to recount his morning, where he had gone, with whom, when he had last opened his wallet, whether he had made any purchases. Her steady interrogating voice gave him something to hold on to, like a stick proffered to a man chest-deep in quicksand. To each question he replied, "I can't think." At last she believed him merely stubborn, a mule with feet planted firmly in the dirt of his own refusal, reveling in it to test her logic and good will.

Suddenly she relented. Of course he would be upset; it was reasonable. He needed her assurance he was not alone in this, that the only person he knew within a five-thousand-mile radius understood his predicament and would come to his aid. If the circumstances were reversed, she would expect consolation. But she, too, had been frightened. Because of that her first impulse had been to abandon him, to leave him in Palermo until he decided he *could* think, and with him the burden of companionship. She could not help contrasting him with the stranger in the bar, a man who surely would not be stopped after a single day abroad. Although she had walked away, she had recognized in that man the hard edge of protection she herself had cultivated; and there was, inevitably, an attraction to the least favored part of the self that found expression in another. As for Harry, she had been unkind and would make it up to him.

As if summoned by Magda's thoughts, the man with the dark shock of hair on his forehead appeared, his face as inscrutable as the stony-eyed gods lining the balustrades at Piazza Pretoria. Leaning over the back of Harry's chair, he dropped three credit cards bearing the name HAROLD D. BAGNOVICH one by one into his lap. To Harry this was a miracle; but Magda, who had come to believe in the industry of invisible hands, was not surprised.

Looking up at the white moon of Harry's face, and, floated above him, the darker one of the man whose body was concealed behind the overstuffed chair, Magda saw them as variations on a theme, like a man and his shadow. For a moment she expected the dark face to descend and align itself with the white one. But Harry, even in his relief, understood at that moment that he and Magda were separate people with separate fates, even though they were traveling together.

III

HARRY HAD VOLUNTEERED TO DRIVE TO AGRIGENTO AS penance for the late start. Taking his camera from under the seat, he checked his pockets for his wallet, reading glasses, and handkerchief. Magda agreed there was something to be said for traveling light, but to cover all bases she packed the many pockets and flaps of a large expensive camera bag with wide-angle and telephoto lenses, extra film and camera batteries, lens paper, a small spiral notebook, pens in three colors, a host of maps and guidebooks, sunglasses with gradient lenses, mineral water in a plastic bottle, a collapsible cup, the Girl Scout knife with the luminous green handle she had carried since fourth grade, granola bars for quick energy and sugarless gum for sudden changes in altitude, lip balm, pressed powder, hairbrush, toothbrush and a tiny tube of toothpaste, dental floss, first-aid kit, several packets of pre-moistened towelettes, travel Kleenex, a sewing kit with four colors of thread and two needles, tiny scissors in the shape of a stork, a black folding umbrella with a duck's head handle, plastic rain hat, a cotton sweater, international driver's license, passport, a solar-powered calculator, money (dollars and lire), travelers checks, credit cards, a black scarab with reputedly sacred inscriptions carved in hieroglyphics on its round stomach, and a medal bearing the likeness of St. Christopher who protected all travelers. She had reviewed the contents, looking for something to jettison, but she could part with nothing. Hoisting the bag to her shoulder, she accepted the price of being prepared.

The Valley of the Temples was not a valley at all but a steep ridge baked hard by the relentless sun. They would have to climb it. There was shade in the lower reaches, under the mimosas, pines, and olive trees they passed. Harry wanted to stop to cool off but felt embarrassed about suggesting it since they had barely begun. Already sweat dampened his shirt in half moons under his arms, and the handkerchief he used to mop his face and neck was soaked.

Parched, treeless, the top of the ridge was the color of sand, nearly the same shade as the nine temples strung across it. Like desert oases, they were spaced at intervals that offered respite at exactly the point where a traveler would have resigned himself to misfortune.

The Temple of Concord was deserted except for nesting birds on the tops of the columns. Magda could not see them but paused on the steps to listen to their incessant song. "An orchestra," she remarked, smiling at Harry.

Because the temple rested on a high foundation, nothing more than blue sky was visible overhead and between the thirty-four tawny columns. Propping her camera bag in a corner, she unbuttoned her collar and rolled up her sleeves to increase her exposure to the sun.

"May I have this dance?" she asked, bowing with mock formality.

"Thanks," said Harry, "but I'll have to sit this one out."

Lowering himself to the floor, he leaned back against the base of a limestone column. Its narrow shadow gave the illusion of shade but provided no relief. Blotting his forehead on his sleeve, he said, "You be the dancer, I'll be your audience."

Although she felt self-conscious, Magda walked to the center of the temple and slowly lifted her arms, placing one hand in the hand of her invisible partner and the other around his waist. The birds she had come to think of as larks, the happiest of birds, encouraged her. Closing her eyes, she imagined the columns still bore their white stucco covering and the frieze was still painted in gaudy reds and blues. In the step-step-close of a ballroom waltz, she made her way across the stone floor worn smooth as the palm of her hand. The more she danced, the more she wanted to dance, like the runner whose true destination is a place fixed in the mind.

An Agrigento tradition required a husband and wife to visit this temple on their wedding day, Magda had read. *Concord* for *harmony*, she thought, as in two voices joined, or *covenant*, as in marriage. Again she was struck by the memory of the wedding she had planned but had been cheated out of. She had engaged the church, a priest, reception hall and caterer, a vocalist with violin accompaniment. She had ordered a tiered cake and armfuls of red anthuriums, their large glossy hearts spiked with spadices where the two lobes meet. These last were to have been flown from a little-remarked-upon island in the West Indies. The wedding would have been small but perfect for she had thought of everything.

A month before the day they were to have become man and wife, Ramon returned to the island to prepare for her arrival. The house that had been his would be theirs to share. He ordered it whitewashed and the low concrete block fence which bordered the road repaired, he hired a water tank installed on stilts so Magda could bathe when the main supply was locked off, he oversaw the woman who scrubbed the speckled tile floors and swept the veranda and dirt yard with long stalks of sugar cane, a woman of no discernable age who wore a pink plastic shower cap and a print dress adorned with a row of safety pins from bodice to hem. She looked unreliable but worked in her own way and at her own pace until she decided Ramon's house was fit for an American wife. Without instructions from him, she arranged birds of paradise in rum bottles and lined the windowsills with colored glass jars. The incense she burned, her own concoction, she knew to be an aphrodisiac although she told Ramon its purpose was to kill the musty odor the house had acquired during his absence. She kept one eye on the weather while she worked, and when the afternoon turned the color of dusk she left without notice. Dust engulfed her on the road home, and she clutched the pouch she wore on a string around her neck, lumpy with fragments of bone and bright bits of feather.

Magda never learned what drew Ramon out into the gale that swept across the tiny island, rearranging in seconds whatever small order had been eked out through decades of hoarding and hard labor. Ninety-mile-an-hour gusts peeled corrugated tin roofs from houses. Airborne, the whirling rectangles of razor-sharp metal slashed down mango and banana trees, and coconut palms whose fruit rolled like heads. Rains flooded the roads and forced cars down the steep sides of mountains and into the sea. In the aftermath, crippled goats lurched blindly over the cliffs and cows lay bloated in the flattened vegetation. All this Magda saw on a videotape that turned up in her mailbox addressed in a round child-like scrawl, no note enclosed.

Alone in her darkened living room, she replayed the tape until she could reconstruct it scene by scene from memory. Grey, statical, blurred by torrential rains and wild camera sweeps, its meaning eluded her. Repeatedly she pushed PAUSE, staring as if she could force the images to relinquish the answer to her question, which hovered, she was certain, just beyond the dimensions of the screen.

Swept out to sea or sucked up into the hurricane's greedy eye, Ramon had disappeared. Without a body to bury there had been no reason for Magda to travel to the island. Had she gone, she would have found nothing except the toppled water tank burst at its seams like an overripe star fruit and a few concrete blocks laced with shards of colored glass. For two years she had counted her losses like Hail Marys on the rosary she no longer carried.

The white dress still hung in her closet. Stuffed with tissue paper, draped on a padded hanger, it looked like a body waiting to be inhabited. And she still wore the ring that meant promise above the gold one she had bought herself when she recited her vows without him.

Magda's hands had grown warm and pulsed as if the air were a body she held. She stopped dancing, not suddenly, but like a wind-up toy gradually run down. Despite the unceremonious close, Harry applauded, the several claps echoing across the valley below. Reminded of his presence, she rolled down her sleeves, rebuttoned her collar, and remarked they must hurry because there were many temples to visit before dusk.

Harry was miserable. His arms were sunburned but not nearly as badly as his face, he knew without looking in a mirror. His legs ached. He was thirsty. His belt cut in under his stomach and restricted his breathing. Soon he dropped behind Magda who walked without apparent effort, her step measured, persistent, robotic even, he thought, as if she were programmed to ignore ordinary human limitations. She read while she walked, her head bent into a guidebook. By an act of will he followed her across the ridge, reaching each temple just as she was preparing to leave. The last temple, the

Temple of Zeus, was so ruined that it looked to Harry like a rock pile on Alcatraz. He found Magda reading beside a telamon that had been reassembled in the center of a large sandy circle. Laid out like a corpse, it was one of the few things that made sense in the rubble. He sat down on its foot, which was about the same height as a chair.

"We can rest, if you like," said Magda, glancing up at his face, which looked red and swollen as if he had been stung. "At least it's all downhill from here."

"That's a misconception," Harry said irritably. "Uphill, downhill, it makes no difference. We still have to exert energy to stop ourselves, otherwise we'd roll down this ridge like those boulders over there. Either way, it's an argument between the body and gravity."

Magda didn't agree. She knew how difficult it was to force ascent when the earth insisted on hugging its own. At junior high school slumber parties the girls begged her to be the one who lay on the floor to be levitated. It never worked with the others who laughed at the crucial moment, but Magda willed herself into a trance they had to coax her out of. She imagined herself as a dead princess supine in a crystal coffin suspended from chains in a dark cave. Folding her arms across her chest she pictured her heart, its ventricles and atriums fed by warm streams of blood; she witnessed its contractions from a place inside herself. Her heart was a plucky horse, galloping across a vast plain. Although it tried to evade her, she lassoed it and made it canter. She longed to draw it down to a halt, and this she knew she could do, but she let it walk.

The other girls knelt around her, each with two fingers V'ed under her body. *Light as a feather, stiff as a board*, they chanted by candlelight. *Light as a feather, stiff as a board. I believe in Mary Worth. I believe in Mary Worth.* Slowly they stood, raising Magda into the air. To the other girls it was a game, but Magda was tantalized by this glimpse into the spirit world where the Mary Worth of slumber party legend lived after the terrible automobile accident that left her disfigured. Maybe, Magda had thought, her own parents lived there, too, along with the martyred saints who had yearned for tragedy to catapult them over the white wall. When she opened her eyes on the ordinary clamor of her friends in shorty pajamas, jumbo pink hair curlers, and furry house slippers, the double-edged sword of scorn and regret cut her to the bone.

Maybe Harry was right, she concluded, both ascent and descent extracted equal payment. Taking the mineral water from her bag she filled her collapsible cup and gave the bottle to him, although she thought he should have come prepared.

Near the exit there was a two-wheeled vendor's cart bedecked with hats in every conceivable style. Those who milled around it were as sunburned as Harry and, like him, were planning for the future a day late. Magda pointed out a jaunty safari hat, but he chose a broad-brimmed Stetson with a leather band encircling the crown. On the way back to the car, he modeled it on his fist. Although the brim turned up he forced it down, concluding the effect was Spanish. In a hat like this, he thought, he would look like a conquistador, a conqueror.

IV

HARRY WORE HIS HAT THE NEXT MORNING, MAGDA could not help but notice, when she glimpsed him through the leaded glass panels in the Hotel Costazzurra's heavy wooden door that she opened to reach the parking lot. Lounging with one foot on the rear bumper, his pose reminded Magda of Oedipus' confident slouch as he shook his finger in the astonished face of the Sphinx in a painting she loved; never mind that her hero stood knee deep in the bones of those who were not good at riddles.

When Harry straightened and turned at her approach, she saw he had printed his name in thick, squat capitals on a five-inch section of the hat's leather band. Although she admired his skillful lettering, she concluded that the gesture was too public, imagining perfect strangers calling him by name as he walked in places he had never been before.

After saluting her by touching two fingers to the brim, Harry took a small tube from his breast pocket and began coating his nose with a white cream, starting at the bridge and carefully working his way down over the tip.

"I'm ready today," he told Magda, replacing the cap with a flourish. "Zinc oxide," he confided, before returning the tube to his pocket, which he patted.

They entered the archaeological zone at Siracusa through a lush garden planted with fragrant trees. Although Magda could not see the grove, she smelled lemons mingled with the sweet scent of oleander along the sandy path. Centuries ago both slaves and masters had walked where she now walked to reach the quarries, where each day was longer than a day. All around her was the bitter evidence of design and execution, of a hierarchy that consigned some men to a palace and others to a prison. This was a place that pulled the past forward, proof no story was ever entirely lost. Out of respect for those who had toiled under the whip, Madga slowed her breath, afraid even the slightest motion would break the spell that had permitted her to balance for a moment on time's quixotic precipice.

"Oranges," Harry said, coming up beside her, thumping his chest and inhaling deeply out of pleasure in the good, clean scent.

Pieces of the picture she had been constructing flew off in all directions like a flock of startled birds.

"Or lemons," she said finally, studying his round face.

He turned to look at her. "How can you tell?" he asked quickly, stepping in front of her on the winding path to avoid colliding with a band of Sicilian children, a bright banner of a dozen or more streaming past as if they had been cut from a single length of cloth, hooting and giddy with freedom at having been sprung from whatever dark interiors had confined them on this sun-drenched day. In the quiet they left in their wake, Harry's question pulled her forward; she followed him as if tied by a rope around her waist.

Around the last curve a huge cavern opened up in front of them. Stone blocks as big as cars had been quarried from the pits and piled around the entrance. In spite of their size they were nearly obscured by trailing vines, maidenhair ferns, and colored lichens. A score of brilliant green lizards sunning themselves on the hot surface scattered when Harry pushed the vines away to show Magda the deep U's cut by the ropes the slaves had used to haul the stones up the cliffs. Thousands of Athenian soldiers had been imprisoned in the quarries after the attack on Siracusa. Having survived the battle and death march, they worked the pits naked, parched, half-starved. They cursed their luck, and then they died.

To Harry the cavern's entrance looked like a drawing of a vagina he had seen in an anatomy book as a boy, his first furtive inquiry into sex. "Fuck," he muttered, trying to imagine the kind of man who could take on a woman like that. He had had a wife who bore him three sons she dropped with ease into the world. They had met at Oberlin College and married while Eisenhower still smiled benignly from the nation's black and white television sets. When their youngest graduated from Kent State holding a political science degree with a concentration in conflict, Harry's wife told him their life together was unsalvageable. Twenty-six years of marriage, more than half of his life, scuttled and sunk in the morass of memory. A good sailor, he had gone down with the ship. Celibate now for four years, he dreamed the vessel restored, its prow cutting deep water.

Leaving Magda near the entrance with her guidebook, he felt his way along the sheer walls curving deeper into the cavern. Sheltered, cool, alone, he reached out with both hands and pressed them against the smooth hewn surface. His palms began to tingle as if he had held them too long in one position. Drawing them back, he rubbed them briskly as if he were trying to start a fire. In the cavern's dim light he imagined flames sparking under his hands, igniting the circuitry of his body, every organ, every appendage, suddenly awake. This is what it must be like, he thought, to enter a woman with your whole body. Furtively, he glanced down at himself to verify the sensation he was afraid to trust. As surprised and grateful as if he had won a lottery without having bought a ticket, he regarded his hands, the wall, the cavern arching overhead, the vine-tangled stones and pale green lizards with darting tongues—not to mention Magda, who dallied somewhere behind him still reading her guidebook, he supposed—the rowdy Sicilian children whose shrill shouts echoed around him, their imperturbable mothers, and even the very air with new and sudden affection.

Outside the sun was straight overhead. Harry squinted in the glare and then took the little tube from his pocket and applied more cream to his nose. Addressing this need made him feel self-sufficient, satisfied, almost grateful for small adversities so he could prove himself dauntless.

Hurrying after Magda who was waiting for him on the sandy path that led to the exit, he saw she had paused beside a grove planted with small trees laden with large yellow fruit. When he stopped beside her, she reached over the wire mesh fence and cupped one in her hand. Tipping it toward him, she said, "Look, they're yellow."

"Yeah, and big as oranges," Harry retorted before he could stop himself. He did not mean to be argumentative for he wanted nothing to dispel his newfound ease that arced over the day. But there she was, Magda-of-the-uncanny-eyes, reciting opinions as if they were divinely inspired.

"For god's sake, Har-ry-Bag-no-vich," she said, enunciating each syllable of his name as if she were reading his hatband, "they're oval, like lemons. Oranges are round." Leaning over the fence and sniffing with authority, she concluded, "Besides, they smell like lemons."

"But some oranges smell like lemons." Again the words tumbled from Harry's lips against his intent and hung in the air out of reach.

Magda looked at him quizzically. Suddenly she laughed and linked her arm through his. Since they were nearly the same height, it was easy to shift her heavy bag from her shoulder to his. "Do you mind?" she asked. "Only for a little while."

The path ended at the archaeological museum, a long, low contemporary structure. It was air-conditioned and Harry pushed off his hat and let it hang down his back, held by a cord around his neck. They began with the cases of impressed pottery brought by sea from the east Mediterranean in the third millennium before Christ and passed through several centuries to arrive at Greek ritual objects. Now they stood before a giant bearded Pan who danced on cloven hooves. His long beard swooped upward. Below, his erection echoed the gesture. When Harry bent down for a closer look, his reflection in the glass slowly aligned itself with the sculpture's hips until Pan's enormous organ appeared to sprout from Harry's head like a horn on a Viking helmet. Startled, Magda stepped back, believing the god had given her a vision that pointed to Harry's true nature, along with a fact that perhaps he himself did not yet know: he was a man who had never really wanted to travel as friends.

When he straightened up, he smiled and looped her camera bag back over her shoulder, which sagged visibly under its weight.

In the car Harry produced a sack of ripe plums he had bought at an outdoor market in Agrigento long before Magda woke. They would be warm, Harry thought, after a day in the hot car. He kidded her about Harry's Ristorante Italiano, so elite it seats only two, and his specialty of the day, baked plums.

"*Mange,*" he said, offering her the sack. Before she could take one, he reached into the bag with his other hand and withdrew two that he rotated in his palm like Chinese exercise balls, admiring their perfect shape and deep purple color. Turning congenially toward her as he took the first bite, juice spurted between his lips, flecking Magda's throat and arm. On a diagonal across her white blouse, just above her left breast, three round stains appeared, brilliant as rubies. Glancing down, she relegated the accident to the second order of miracles: blood without a wound.

Harry was sorry, his apologies profuse. He took out his handkerchief and moved as if to blot the stains, but Magda leaned hard against the passenger door as if held by the kind of force that pins thrill seekers in their seats on roller coasters. Because he did not know what else to do, he put the key in the ignition, started the car, and pulled out onto the road toward Taorima.

Out of the corner of his eye, he glanced again at the three drops that led his eye toward Magda's nipple. He imagined it sweet, the color of plums. Her breasts were small, he could tell, unlike those of the headless stone goddess he had admired in the archaeological museum. Mother to twins, one infant cradled in each arm, the goddess nursed her darlings in perpetuity, an eager mouth fastened to each pendulous breast. After photographing her from several angles, Harry bought the postcard in the museum shop in case his slides were not what he hoped.

V

STILL MILES AWAY, HARRY WAS THE FIRST TO DETECT the faint plume rising from Etna's central crater, and it was he who first discerned the volcano's vague outline suffused with haze and clouds. Magda would have missed these early almost magical glimpses if she had been traveling alone.

They circled up the spur of Mount Tauro to the hilltop city of Taorima then spiraled down the other side where the road began its ascent toward Etna. In the distance the peak looked small, harmless, although traces of lava were visible along the road between patches of weedy moss that bore tiny pink tubular flowers.

"How pretty," said Magda, her way of asking Harry to pull over so she could photograph the blossoms with her macro lens.

"I suppose," he said, turning onto the shoulder, "but think about it." He paused.

"Well?" asked Magda, getting out of the car.

"Volcanology," Harry called, walking around to her side. "Sure, it's pretty on the surface. Flowers, trees," he gestured vaguely, "it's easy to forget all that seething under there. It goes down probably for miles, just boiling away deep in some crack and then..." He made churning motions with both hands to complete his sentence. "Really, it can erupt any time."

Magda took off her sunglasses and studied him for a moment before she knelt, adjusted the lens, and shot his foot wreathed with pink blooms. Above her, Harry studied her vertebrae outlined against the thin fabric of the white blouse stretched across her back. He thought of her spine flexing and of the bony cage of her ribs holding her like arms. Again he thought past the protocol of clothes she would have him believe comprised the whole Magda, as if a cross section would reveal nothing more than the skirts and blouses she wore, always white or black, nested one inside the other like Russian dolls. Standing over her, looking down at the small bones in her wrists syncopating as she rewound the film, he was moved by her faith in human endeavor. Even here, amid the reminders of a devastation that proved such belief was perverse, she sought out and recorded beauty.

On the mineral-rich lower slopes they passed groves of oranges, lemons, pistachios and almonds, olive trees by the hundreds, and miles of tended vineyards. As the ascent gradually grew steeper, these gave way to stands of oak, beech, birch, and pine. Higher up the vegetation thinned and then ceased. The slopes were riddled with fist-sized chunks of lava and the landscape became desolate, as if the journey Magda and Harry had started had become a different journey, one they had not intended to take.

Harry had to watch the road, which now wound steeply upward and was separated from the sheer rock face only by a flimsy railing. Staring out the window, Magda tried to hold her eyes on the straight line of the horizon and pretend she was out there on that level plain instead of in the car beside Harry who drove, she believed, too fast and too close to the edge.

The guardrail was dented in too many places to count. Magda imagined terror washing like a tidal wave over those travelers who braked against the thin metal they prayed would save their lives even while nodding to the temptation of empty space, of pure sky that hypnotized them with a promise they would realize too late it could not keep. In one place the railing was shattered and sections lay scattered below. Someone had erected a crude wooden cross to mark the tragedy. Harry put on the emergency brake when he got out to take pictures of the twisted metal and the two sticks bound with twine. When he returned, he put one hand on her knee and said, "We're almost there."

The air had grown cold. When they stopped at Rifugio Sapienza to transfer to the jeep that would take them to the top, Harry retrieved the windbreaker he had carried along in the trunk. Magda pulled her sweater from her camera bag and buttoned it up to her neck. The driver spoke no English so Harry asked him questions about the depth of the crater, its width, the frequency of eruption, first in the Portuguese he had learned in Brazil during a stint with the Peace Corps and then, noting the man's blank stare, in high school Spanish.

He talked with dogged persistence until Magda put her hand on his arm and said kindly, "Harry, Portuguese is not Italian, Spanish is not Italian, and no combination of Portuguese and Spanish can ever be Italian."

"Then I'll learn Italian," he replied quietly.

They drove the rest of the way in silence. The driver sped up the road with a savage velocity even Harry never would have dared. He took the curves without slowing, and Magda found herself flung against Harry, shoulder to thigh. Helpless with vertigo, she could not pull away. Closing her eyes, she invoked St. Christopher and delivered herself into his hands.

Without warning the driver jolted to a stop and made them understand this was as far as they would go. Why, Magda wanted to know, since the plateau was some distance from the top. Again Harry tried to question the guide who simply shrugged. He motioned them from the jeep then pointed to their cameras and waved at the eddies of black lava frozen into broad streams and the rumpled torrents halted mid-wave. In places it welled up into formations the size of cottages. Life-sized figures hunched in every direction as if they slept under a spell. Hundreds of blackened cones turned the landscape into an immense kingdom that sloped in every direction for as far as the eye could see. No bird or insect, nothing could live here.

"Lunar," said Harry.

But Magda thought of underwater reefs, winding coral in an endless sea, spiny black Caribbean coral, staghorn, mushroom, and brain coral, deeply fissured and magnified to the right scale for Polyphemus who had a taste for the flesh of men, especially those who nosed around the fiery crater he called home. Blind, enraged, it was from here he had flung boulders at Odysseus who was safely out at sea, Odysseus who, in an act of boundless pride, shouted back his name to claim the credit he believed he deserved. Then the giant was alone again, nursing his bloody eye. Magda pitied him as she did any strong thing brought down.

A cold rain started up. Her rain hat and umbrella were no comfort against the chill. The sky was dark and the air thick with the smell of sulfur. Harry ventured over to the rim of one of the smaller craters and peered in. Layers of blackness concealed its floor. Taking up a chunk of lava, he pitched it into the crater's center and cocked his head to listen, but no sound broke the eerie silence.

"Jesus," he said, "they'd have a hell of a time hauling a body out of there. You'd have to write it off like a burial at sea."

"That's how I think of it," she said suddenly, "as a sea."

Although Harry still must have been nearby, Magda could not see him through the twists of smoke and mist swirling like wraiths around them. She imagined them as the spirits of all those who had been swept away in the sea of molten lava. Somewhere not too far above her the immense cauldron of the central crater seethed. She longed for an aerial view that would reveal the burning eye and black rivers fanning the crater's flanks and point out her place in the scheme of things.

She had not come this far, she thought bitterly, to be denied the edge that would suspend her between a measureless height and a measureless depth. In that one moment, poised on such an edge, she knew the spinning world would stabilize and meaning would materialize as surely as Harry's name printed in black ink across the leather band of his hat. So this is what Hell is like, she thought, fingering the edge of the formation beside her, sharp enough to flay her flesh in an instant. Like St. Bartholomew, she thought, who carried his skin draped like a coat over one arm on his journey across the walls of Italy's great cathedrals.

The sudden but slight pressure on her shoulders did not startle her. Somehow familiar, predictable even, it was a thing she leaned into. This was the moment she had suffered into being. *The spirit made flesh.* It had happened before. She whirled around, expecting a flash of radiance to illuminate this blasted landscape and set down the body of the man she carried in her heart. Already her lips were shaping the soft iamb of his name — *Ramon.* Instead it was Harry she faced, Harry who had taken off his jacket and draped it around her, Harry who mistook her confusion for concern that now he, too, would be cold.

VI

HARRY DROVE THE CAR ONTO THE FERRY AT MESSINA for the short trip across the Strait to Reggio di Calabria on the mainland. On deck they leaned against the railing, and Magda read aloud how it was here in this Strait where Charbydis sucked generations of sailors into her great watery pit. Harry watched the fishing boats. Harpoons in hand, the fishermen rode long booms out over the water scanning the sea for swordfish. Later Magda and Harry would see these same fish hacked to bits on bloody tables in the open air markets, their heads mounted above the stalls, their long noses pointing like arrows toward the vacant sky.

After Harry claimed the car and checked it over for damage, Magda insisted on driving, saying she felt guilty for not doing her share.

The road to Sorrento was choked with heat and smoke blown from the fields. "The fires must have been set," said Harry. "Burn-off, like the prairies."

Magda looked around at the dry yellow grass and scorched foliage. "They could have started by themselves," she ventured.

"How's that?" asked Harry, thinking he must have missed a word or two.

"You know, spontaneous combustion. It happens. There've been cases where a person's burst into flames," she said, growing more certain of her theory with each word. She imagined a match lit in another world and carried down to this one pinched between a giant thumb and forefinger. The gears ground when she downshifted to get a better look at the fields. To Harry the sound was an insult and this, he calculated, was the third time in nearly as many miles.

"Look, I don't mind driving. It'll give you a chance to watch the scenery," he said, falling silent when she did not answer. He knew it was futile to press her for examples of people combusting, although he felt dangerously close himself.

A hundred miles into the Appenines she still mistook one gear for another although, as he finally pointed out, the shifting pattern was plainly printed on the knob. He tried to explain the most economical gears for the hilly terrain and how to ease the clutch instead of popping it. Whether she could not or would not understand, he did not know, but her senseless abuse of a good machine made him angry.

"Do you have any idea what that does to the transmission?" he asked irritably, but she failed to answer.

The road was riddled with tunnels, some of them miles long, cut right through the mountains. After the first few, Magda complained that she could not see, that she felt blinded by the sudden shifts from light to dark.

"I close my eyes before we reach the entrance," he told her, "so they'll have time to adjust. Otherwise I couldn't see anything either."

"Harry, I'm driving!"

"I'll spell you for awhile," he offered, amused by his transparent ruse.

By the time they counted the fourteenth tunnel, Harry's eyes burned from the carbon monoxide, even though huge fans mounted on the ceiling propelled the poison fumes toward the exit. Magda said she could feel the burn in her throat and deeper down in her lungs. "It's invasive," she said.

"Maybe like sex with a person you don't like," Harry replied, listening to each syllable fall like a stone in a landslide of impulse and bad judgment. He felt like a stranger even to himself. When he saw Magda stiffen, he wished he could retrieve his words from the wreckage at the bottom of conversation's rocky slope, swallow them back, and set down new ones like a path through an orderly garden he could follow to reach her. He had only wanted to talk, to find an avenue around the wall of secrecy she had built for her own reasons brick by brick between them. Now, again, he was assured there would be no more talk for miles.

"I'm hot," she said, when she finally broke the silence. "Will you help me off with this sweater so I don't have to pull over?" She had been fussing with her sweater for an hour, pushing it down over her shoulders and pulling it up again as they drove through alternating patches of cool mountain air and insufferable hot spots. Now she was suffocating, she told Harry, and she wanted it off. He reached behind her and guided her arms out through the sleeves, careful not to touch her bare skin.

In the last long tunnel on the outskirts of Sorrento, they saw lines of cars parked on both sides of the road. "Check the guidebook, will you?" she asked, braking, thinking she had overlooked some attraction.

But Harry noticed the squares of cardboard covering the steamed-up windows and how the cars rocked on their struts. He laughed and said, "But the show's right here."

The Hotel Cocumello used to be a Jesuit monastery, the brochure said. Magda's room was small but no longer monastic. The sleeping chamber was separated from an alcove by a long lace curtain she could open and close by pulling a rope with a heavy wooden ball attached to the end. In the alcove were French doors opening onto a garden with tall umbrella pines that framed a triangle of deep blue sea. When she opened the doors as some robed and sandaled monk must have done each evening years ago, the Tyrrhenian breeze cooled the thick concrete walls and tile floor.

Harry sat in the lobby and studied the Italian phrase book he had bought while he waited for Magda to come down for dinner. Later, in the trattoria, he said, "Let me order. For practice." And, in fact, the waiter brought the bowl of steaming spaghetti with mussels, the grilled swordfish, green salad, and the bottle of dry white wine she had told Harry she wanted.

"Tell me about your room," she said, "in English, please," and then she laughed, fine lines gathering around her eyes. Since they had arrived in Sorrento, Harry had come to think of the blue part of her eye as Tyrrhenian blue.

"It's in the new wing. Cheap construction," he said, pocketing his reading glasses. "Tacked on to take advantage of the tourist dollar, and there's one tiny window that overlooks the parking lot. Hotter than hell in there and no air-conditioning, not even a fan." Harry spoke of the adversity with enthusiasm, so elated he was to encounter again the smiling woman who had linked her arm through his in Palmero that first night. "How did you fare?" he asked.

She told him her room was in the old part and mentioned the French doors but not the view or the breeze, and not the arches that rose like a canopy above the bed or the intricately patterned tile floor—nothing else, in fact, at all.

In Italian Harry asked for the bill, and in Italian he read each of the six digits aloud when it came. When Magda reached for her bag, he said, "My treat," and fanned the colorful lire across the table. Outside he offered her his arm in a gesture of exaggerated chivalry for the walk back to the hotel, an arm she accepted in the spirit in which it was given.

Harry wanted to explore the garden while he waited for his room to cool down, but Magda begged off. Closing the heavy door of her room behind her, she felt secluded but at the same time open to the world. The moon bathed the room with a perfect light she watched through the French doors while she undressed. Slipping between the stiff white sheets, she felt pure as a nun.

In her dream she slept beside Ramon, the man she would always love. Her arm flung across his chest was barely distinguishable since his skin was olive like her own. He told her in Italian he had traveled a great distance from an island he called Sorrento where the warm caressing air was thick with the smells of flowering and decay. They rose from the bed to dress themselves in gauzy white saris, for they were to be married and make of their flesh one flesh. The bells rang softly at first and then clanged stridently. When Magda woke the bells of San Francesco were still chiming.

She closed the French doors and slept again in an attempt to find that same man among the thousands who could enter her dreams. But this time she walked a rocky coast that threatened to pitch her into the sea with each step. The drop was treacherous and rocks the size of skulls were strewn down the slope. When she stumbled, a hand appeared to help her. The fingers opened one by one and then closed around hers. Although the hand was larger than hers, it appeared grafted onto her wrist so similar were their complexions. Lifting her eyes in anticipation, she was greeted by Harry's white face. The inverted *V* of even whiter zinc oxide coating his nose made it look as though death had eaten it away. As for the rocks, she saw they had been skulls all along.

After Magda returned to her room, Harry went down to the garden alone. The cool night air refreshed him, and he unbuttoned his shirt to the waist. Sitting down on a stone bench supported by a pair of crouching sphinxes, he opened his phrase book to THE PARTS OF THE BODY. *La mano*, he read by moonlight, and beneath it *la testa* and *il cuore*. "Hand, head, heart," he repeated out loud as he looked up at the same moon Magda watched from her room. Then he turned back toward the hotel hunting with his eyes for the French doors she had described at dinner. He saw them at once. Every day he had studied her clothing, the varying lengths of her sleeves and skirts. Her body, he thought, when he imagined her undressing, would be tanned in increments, like a map guiding him to the white center.

His room was as hot as the sun-baked ridge at Agrigento, and the air lay on his body like a wet sheet. He slept naked and dreamed in Italian. The words slid from his tongue perfect as pearls when he spoke to a cluster of dark, smiling women who nodded their full assent after each sentence. They adored him, he knew, for he had charmed them with his fluency. They pushed back the brim of his hat and kissed his cheek—*la guancia*, his chest and chin—*il torace, il mento*. Madga sat in a corner dressed in a gown the color of the moon. It was then he realized he could tell her anything without fear of reprisal because she alone in the room was without language.

When he woke he heard himself repeating *la guancia, il torace, il mento,* although these were not the words he had memorized. He picked up his phrase book where it had fallen beside the bed to check the translations. The words must have come, he concluded, from a place inside him where all knowledge resided. He felt wise, like a prophet.

VII

THE STREETS OF POMPEII WERE PAVED WITH STONE blocks worn smooth by centuries of wear before Vesuvius buried the city under tons of sorrow. Harry and Magda had barely entered the excavated city when Magda stopped to study a carving cut deep in the stone. She had been puzzling over the identical carving repeated every ten or fifteen meters since they first walked through the gates. It meant something she did not understand, and the guidebook was no help. Nudging Harry, who was reloading his camera, she pointed at the carving with the toe of her sneaker. Kneeling, he checked the light meter one last time, lay down on the warm pavement, and began to shoot.

"They're signs," he told her, in response to her unspoken question.

"Of what?" she wanted to know.

"Even an illiterate could follow them straight to the whorehouse."

"But there must be other possibilities," Magda said. "Maybe they're some kind of talisman. You know, to ward off evil or bring good luck."

"Right," he said, smiling. "Lucky charms."

The house called Lupanare consisted of many tiny rooms, each nearly filled by a high stone bed with a raised stone pillow at one end. Magda preferred to believe the house had belonged to a family with many children, but Harry pointed to the faded frescos adorning the walls. They showed naked men and women locked in every conceivable position, always the man entering the woman. "There you have it," he said, shrugging slowly at the incontestable proof.

Magda went on ahead, leaving him to puzzle out the best camera adjustments for low light. Later, when he met her at the exit, she was standing with her back to the most remarkable fresco he had seen yet. High on the wall above her was a life-sized figure of a man who had hitched up his pale yellow toga with one hand to reveal a penis as long and thick as an arm. In his other hand he held a scale: a sack of rocks filled one dish and his penis filled the other. The scale was perfectly balanced.

"Get a load of this," Harry said, pointing again. Turning, she looked up at the man's helmeted head, his bearded face, and then quickly moved her eyes down to his calf-length boots.

"I'd take the rocks," she said. "He should be stoned."

"Ouch!" said Harry, slumping and pressing his knees together in mock terror. "Move a little to the left and I'll get your photograph," he joked, waving her closer to the fresco. He was trying to goad her into inching away from the confining world of high collars and toward an acknowledgment of the desire he believed she was intent on repressing. But Magda simply walked out of the picture.

Beside the house there was a souvenir stand with postcards on a wire rack that Magda spun while Harry thumbed through a book that reproduced the frescoes they had just seen. The book's small black and white line drawings were accompanied by extensive text, and he told Magda that he would buy the Italian edition as a learning aid. At the last minute, though, he changed his mind and took a version entitled *Forbidden Pompeii* crammed with glossy color photographs of the most intriguing poses.

Magda chose postcards that showed angels drifting in a pale blue sky and winged cupids in chariots pulled by dolphins. In her favorite, a woman who reminded Magda of Rapunzel leaned out of a high tower. Her lover, standing on a nearby precipice, looked up at the woman with longing. Above them hovered a wingless angel who looked like an ordinary woman. When she took their outstretched hands in hers, through her the lovers on their separate heights were joined. Magda studied this card longer than the others for it bore the most hopeful message: a promise of help, an intermediary for those in need.

After she paid for the cards, Magda lingered beside the kiosk, saying she did not want to go any further until she had mapped out their route through the dead city. Taking her red pen from her bag, she drew a line connecting the temples, baths, forums, and theatres she did not want to miss. "Each possesses its own special mystery," she told Harry.

He had a different approach. "Let's just walk," he said, "until we see something that interests us. Then we'll figure out where we are and what it is." As if to illustrate his preference, he stopped in front of an iron-gated shed that housed rows of urns and pots, vessels of every kind salvaged by the hundreds and stacked on crude wooden shelves that bowed under their weight. There were pediments, entablatures, columns, and tympanums in fragments or partially reassembled, and basins, statues, and pedestals enough to rebuild a city. "Amazing," he said. "The world's biggest jigsaw puzzle," he marveled, laughing.

Because Magda could not separate the rubble she saw in front of her from a vision of a past in which each piece was whole and secure, she found the display tragic, even though it was a testament to the art of salvage.

Near the end of the block-long shed they found plaster casts of men, women, and dogs captured in attitudes of flight as they tried to outrun the lava that gushed down Vesuvius' slopes, burying them alive. One woman squatted with her hands clasped near her face as if she were praying or about to stifle a scream of such import it required both hands to suppress. A dog, the chain it had tried to bite through still dangling from its mouth, sprawled with legs stuck out in four directions. They had all watched the lava roar toward them and they knew death was certain, but none suspected their last gesture would be preserved under ash for two thousand years or that they would be what they were forever.

With her telephoto lens Madga shot close-ups of the faces, which seemed to her curiously contemporary. One man, she thought, looked like the proprietor of the corner store in her neighborhood. He had a large hooked nose and one eye was open wide while the other was squinched shut. His full lips were parted as if he intended to speak, but what, after all, she wondered, was left to say. Or maybe he had been napping, breathing through his open mouth, when the lava overwhelmed him like sleep. Maybe he had had only enough time to force one eye back into focus before he was touched in a rare moment by the hands of three realities: dream, waking, and death. Magda continued to photograph his face, hoping to glimpse what he had learned when she studied her developed slides.

For eight hours, the length of a hard day's work, Harry pointed out, they had walked the treeless city in sun he had come to regard as inimical. His hat and the zinc oxide were no match for the sun he swore he would never grow used to. Even Magda's face, arms, and legs were burned a rich red-brown like the Pompeiian red in the whorehouse frescoes. The contrast made the blue part of her eye even more startling, as if it were transplanted from a donor of different race. He thought of the bronze bust of Diana he had photographed in some temple or another with one eye oxidized bright green as if to call attention to her divided self. Diana, Magda had told him, was at home in every realm — in the sky, on earth, and in the lower reaches. In an instant she could transform herself from the Goddess of the Dark of the Moon, whose magic knew no bounds, into the pure Maiden-Goddess, who bathed the world with her chaste light. Among all the gods, it was she who most readily navigated between good and evil.

"Let's call it a day," Harry said, sinking down on the ledge of an empty rectangular pool.

"Do you know what you're sitting on?" Magda asked, turning the page in her guidebook.

"I'm too hungry to care."

"It's a vat. This is Fullonica Stephani, a laundry. They washed their clothes in these vats. They trampled them clean in water and soda or urine." Magda thought this was the kind of earthy detail that would appeal to Harry and persuade him to stay a little longer.

"Jesus," he said, "piss. Let's eat."

Closing her guidebook, she looked down at him still sitting on the ledge and saw he had stuck two feathers in his hatband, one on each side of his name, exceptional wing-shaped feathers fit for the heels of Mercury.

Harry went into the first trattoria he spotted without asking Magda's opinion. When the platter of mixed fried seafood he had ordered arrived, a small whole fish crowned the jumble. He prodded it with his fork.

"Looks like a goldfish," Magda said, leaning across the table.

"Right," said Harry. "THE GOLDFISH. ITALY'S NATIONAL DISH," he announced as if he were reading a newspaper headline.

Peering at her over the top of his glasses, he picked up the fish with his fingers and bit a hole in its side. "Tasty," he said, quickly eating it down to the skeleton. Magda watched as he sucked the index finger of his right hand and then the index finger of his left hand, the middle finger of his left hand and then the middle finger of his right, alternating in this manner until he had sucked every finger. The quick motion reminded her of someone playing a polka on the mouth organ.

Untangling a round carcass the size of a ping-pong ball, he held it up for inspection. "Octopus," he reported. "Try one," he offered.

"I have enough."

"Thanks," she said, "but no. This salad is enough for me. It's got everything I like." She glanced at the tomatoes, shredded carrots, and bitter green olives.

"Just one," he urged, holding it out to her. Tentacles sprawling, it looked like a miniature Medusa's head aloft in the hand of Perseus.

"Oh, maybe later," she said, waving it away.

"Then a small piece," he said, pulling off a tentacle and parting his own lips to encourage her.

In spite of herself, she opened her mouth. She felt his fingers on her tongue when he put it inside. They were warm, smooth, and tasted of oil and salt.

It was late by the time they returned to Sorrento. Harry drove and Magda reclined her seat and slept. Glancing at her, he felt protective although he could not have said why, and close behind, the urge to touch her. How much could he touch, he wondered, before she woke. He looked at the curve of her neck where her head tilted to one side, at her shoulder, which must be cruelly marked by the heavy camera bag he could not talk her into leaving behind, at the slight rise and fall of her breast where he dared not look when he had splattered her blouse with the three startling drops of plum juice, and at her fragile hand, palm up on the seat beside him.

Again he was struck by how little he knew of her apart from whatever brief history they had forged. How could they have traveled as friends, he wondered, for they had not been friends, they had barely been acquainted. Yes, there had been the photography class but they had talked f-stops and apertures, and the few visits to her house had offered no clues. A Spanish colonial with white rooms and bare wood floors, walls of rough plaster, unadorned, the few pieces of furniture functional. It was as if a criminal had moved in and removed all traces of a former guilty life. Harry wanted her to relent, let down her guard and take him in, for he believed himself a good man worthy of her trust, of even more, he would have admitted had he been honest with himself.

Magda did not wake until he opened her car door in the hotel parking lot. Although he was dead tired and believed his sunburn was serious enough to require medical attention, he walked Magda to the lobby then went down to the bar in the garden. He ordered from a surly waiter who suggested, in English, a fine German beer or even, perhaps, American. No, Harry insisted in Italian, he wanted the beer of the region. After his third glass he still ordered in Italian, and the waiter still replied in English.

"Fuck," he muttered when he opened the door to his room, "a fucking blast furnace." Stripping off his clothes, he lay naked on the bed and opened the book he had bought at Pompeii. The first plate showed a swarthy man leaning against a pillar to support the woman whose legs were wrapped around his waist. Turning to the caption, he read several sentences before he realized his mistake. The text was in French, not the language in which he dreamed.

VIII

MAGDA WOKE UP EARLY, REFRESHED, AND OPENED the French doors. At her feet hundreds of ants swarmed over the carcass of a dead wasp. Methodically, with the ball of her foot, she crushed them, moving from left to right as if she were reading.

Kneeling to brush them over the edge, she noticed a makeshift exercise room on the monastery's porch one floor below that had been glassed in as part of the renovation. The lower torso of a man moved into view, but the angle prevented her from seeing his face. His olive skin glistened with exertion, and the weight he lifted brought the muscles in his bare stomach and thighs into clear definition. Magda ducked back into her room and pushed the doors closed with her foot. She hurried down to breakfast, hoping Harry would be waiting. When he did not appear, she phoned his room.

"*Pronto*," he answered, his voice dopey with sleep.

"Harry?"

Rarely had she called him by name. The soft syllables in her mouth caused him to imagine what it would be like to wake up beside her. "*Pronto*," he said again.

"What are you trying to say?" she asked impatiently.

"I'm trying to get you to repeat my name."

The drive from Sorrento to Paestum would require two hours, not one, as Magda had estimated. Harry's neck already hurt and his back ached from the contour of the seat, which, he said, held nothing in common with his body. "But you're such a good driver, Harry," she said. She said, "Harry, you have my complete confidence," and "I feel as secure, Harry, as if I were driving myself." He knew she was teasing him, and that he would have to tolerate it as penance for his sleep-drunk admission that morning.

Ahead of them a three-wheeled vehicle chugged slowly up an incline. Harry honked once but the contraption held the center of the narrow road. He honked again, three times in rapid succession, but again there was no response.

"Look," Magda said, pointing, "they're nuns."

"Fuck the nuns," he muttered, passing them on a hairpin curve.

Magda held her breath as the car swerved but said nothing. That Harry would speak uncensored, knowing she would disapprove, somehow pleased her with its implication of camaraderie. Turning toward the window, she leaned back in her seat and watched the countryside slip by.

Thick nets rolled into tubes were strung between the roadside trees. Some were black, others rust colored. Workers unfurled them to catch the thousands of oranges and lemons that fell from the terraced groves banking the hillside. Harry marveled at the ingenuity that permitted such salvage and at the terraces themselves that turned space Americans would write off as untillable into profit.

Before long they were lost. "It proves your point about failed American ingenuity," Magda said, but she meant it kindly.

"It proves a point, all right. A point about the stupidity of the Italians."

"The Italians are stupid because *you're* lost?" Magda chided.

"*We're* lost, my friend." Harry twisted his head from side to side and twitched his shoulders to work out the cricks. "Anyway, how smart do you have to be to post a few accurate road signs? Road signs are an international courtesy, a matter of foreign policy. People don't have to come to Italy where signs that point left mean straight ahead. They could go somewhere else."

"Where?" she asked, smiling slightly.

"Anywhere. Portugal, for example," he answered, refusing to laugh at himself.

"Portugal? If we were in Portugal right now, we'd be lost all the same."

Pulling onto the shoulder, Harry put one hand on each knee and stared straight ahead. In profile he looked like a bas-relief of an Assyrian king. He had enjoyed their talk about the terraces, but at this moment he regarded Magda's mind as a virulent buzzing nest he had unwittingly disturbed. Every word stung, and now what he wanted was silence.

"But we don't have to be lost," she continued, pointing to a roadside stand heaped with oranges and lemons. "We can ask directions."

"Or we can find our own way. We could spend all day asking directions and never get a straight answer," Harry retorted.

"Or we could spend all day hunting for the right road and get to Paestum after the museum closes."

With a gesture of resignation he opened the car door and strode toward the stand he imagined upending like Christ among the tables of the moneychangers. Although he heard Magda following him, he did not wait for her.

She listened as he greeted the vendor and began asking for directions. Soon she was able to pick out isolated phrases and match them up with the vendor's gestures. Harry mimicked the man's active hands and repeated key words, rolling his r's with an energy and pleasure that restored his inherent good will. Somehow Magda believed she, too, understood the conversation, just as she understood that she could not have set out in the car and driven the route the vendor had mapped in the air without Harry.

In the museum Harry dallied by shards of pottery Magda quickly passed to make her way to the Greek funerary paintings. The tombs lined a long, modern, temperature-controlled gallery with sensors on the walls. The sides and lids were covered with scenes of conveyance —horses and chariots or gondolas rowing the dead to the next world. In the one Magda chose to photograph, a diver was suspended between a white sky and pale green sea. Although he had already sprung from the high stone tower, his feet jutted out as if he were still standing. He gazed into space, not down at the water he would never enter. His body was slender, naked, red-brown, a smooth crescent attached to nothing, like the moon.

Using her body as a tripod, she spread her legs to distribute her weight evenly on both feet and braced her elbows in a *V* against her chest. The lens zoomed in on the diver's face, closing the distance between them in an instant. Magda was entranced by his serene expression, as if his leap were an act of joy. Death had not chosen him; he had chosen it.

Alone in the gallery, she felt he was her diver. He, too, was a traveler, a kindred spirit. Holding her breath, she pressed the shutter several times in rapid succession, then shifted her weight and shot again. The voice at her side startled her and the camera jerked, blurring the shot she had carefully composed.

"I've been watching you," Harry said. "Not here, but from down there." He gestured toward a long hall that led back to the museum's entrance. "First I saw you focus, and then I saw you shift your weight."

In spite of his resolve to keep his little secret, he confessed to Magda the time he had spent observing her while he remained unseen, a favor granted by technology's indiscriminate god. Out of sight, at his leisure, Harry had studied the angle of her head and elbows, the tension in her back and calves as she steadied the camera, and the slow rise of her shoulders to accommodate the breath she would hold while she pressed the shutter. Of course he had glanced at her as she slept in the car while he drove back from Pompeii, but this was different; although her guard was down all the same, here he had observed her at work, reasoning, planning, while harboring the illusion of solitary passage even as he held her in his gaze. Harry's respect for the care with which she framed each shot argued with his delight in catching her unawares.

In reply to the flush inching up past Magda's high white collar, he turned and pointed to the monitor in the corner where his own finger pointed back at him.

It was late afternoon when they returned to the hotel, too late, Harry said, to swim. Alone, Magda walked through the long rock-faced tunnel that led to the public beach. It spiraled down so sharply she had to brace herself to keep from breaking into a run. Recalling

Harry's adamance when they had argued about the difficulties of descent, she smiled to herself over the fact she had been slow to accept. She felt content, walking in the gathering dusk down toward the crescent of black sand that glittered like crushed lava.

Dragging a low-slung canvas chair to the water's edge, she sat on shore and rested her legs in the shallows. Although the beach had been deserted when she arrived, soon a band of scrawny children herded by two blue-aproned nuns descended like Indians whooping it up in an old movie. Turning to watch them, she saw at the top of the cliff a small figure she recognized by the Stetson profiled against the sky. Even when Harry leaned forward with both arms on the railing, she knew he could not see her in the glare of the sun setting over the water. She felt safe from his gaze but also connected to him, as if the vines trailing down the rocky face bound them like cords, wrist to wrist. Her eyes closed involuntarily, and she slept.

When she woke she turned to look for Harry, expecting to find him where he last stood. Although it was nearly dark she could see he had gone. The sea was calm, gray, opaque. She waded out a few meters, then turned and followed the coast. The bottom was rocky but the stones were smooth. They hurt her feet in a way that she accepted. Stooping slightly, she trailed her fingers across the surface with the orchestrated gesture of someone who feels watched. Her outstretched arm looked to her like a stranger's in the half-light that defined and clarified. She waded out further. The water was warm, almost tropical.

Eyes shut tight against the salt sting, toes curled around the stones, she dove and swam underwater until her lungs forced her up. Standing for a moment, she watched the water ripple down the front of her bathing suit. Unbidden, the word came to her: *fiume*, meaning river. Repeatedly, she dove as if she had a destination, as if one time the ending would be different.

The streets of Sorrento that night were brightly lit and nearly impassable since the town was celebrating the festival day for St. Carmelli. Vendors sold cotton candy, popcorn, prunes, sticky confections in neon yellow and green, and holy cards bearing the benign face of the saint. Across the street from the church a brass band struck up, and there were games of chance, pony rides, and a Ferris wheel and tilt-a-whirl illuminated by colored spotlights. The church itself was decorated with strings of Christmas lights and banners. Harry told Magda the scene reminded him of the carnivals he had loved as a boy in Ohio. He described the two-headed baby in a jar of formaldehyde, the hermaphrodite, and the hawker who sold chameleons to affix to a collar or lapel with a stickpin where they wriggled for a day furiously changing color before they died. To Magda it was attractively Catholic, although Harry called it an afternoon of family fun.

Deep in talk, they did not see the black Alfa Romeo parked in a place of privilege in front of the church's double arched doors until they stood beside it. Harry stooped to look inside, but the car was empty except for the usual clutter of travel.

IX

THE PURPLE TRUMPETS OF THE MORNING GLORIES cascaded down the cliffs along the Amalfi Coast into the Vallone di Furore, a deep gorge battered by the sea. Through her camera Magda watched a black bee enter a flower. Adjusting the lens, she pulled the insect close enough to see the separate hairs on its body and its sucking mouthparts, and then she pushed it back until it became an unidentifiable speck.

When she looked up, she saw Harry's camera focused on her. In the museum at Paestum she had felt betrayed by Harry's spying, but now she wondered how many shots he had taken, in what compositions, and whether the slides would show her to her best advantage. She wondered what he would think when he saw her projected on the finely textured screen in his darkened living room, whether he would wish he could call her down to sit beside him. Months or even years later she would appear just as she looked now whenever he flipped the switch.

At breakfast she had read an article in her guidebook describing the frightening hairpin turns and sheer drops along the corniche between Sorrento and Salerno. One man, she told Harry, had sued his travel agent for failing to warn him about the downward glance that prompted his heart attack. But Harry pointed out that the wire nets binding the boulders to the cliffs and the stone barricades would sooner wreck a car than permit it to plunge into the sea.

He must have just missed her at breakfast, he told her, describing the table for two in front of an open window where she must have sat alone. There were crumbs from a crusty roll scattered on the white tablecloth, a small, half-empty pot of strawberry jam, and a glass with a few drops of orange juice in the bottom. She had been reading, he said he had concluded, because the plate had been pushed aside to make room for something the size of the guidebook she now held.

"You're quite the detective," she remarked, admiring his accuracy. He did not tell her he had signaled the waiter to refill her glass or that he drank from the place where her lips had marked the rim.

Amalfi's Duomo Sant' Andrea, built high at the top of a set of broad stairs, looked out over the town. The facade, Magda said, was noted for its elaborate geometric design worked in multicolored stone. Harry was eager to see the crypt, which held the headless body of St. Andrew looted from Byzantium. He read aloud in Italian from a small card near the door that told how the saint's body exuded a holy oil, harbinger of miracles.

A guard seated on a chair at the entrance spoke in rapid Italian about St. Andrew and pointed the way. When he saw they seemed uncertain, he personally led them side-by-side down the nave.

"He wants us to admire his favorite saint," Harry whispered, "so he can reduce his time in purgatory. That's how Catholicism works. He'll show us something most tourists don't see, but of course he'll want a tip."

In spite of his cynicism, Harry was eager to follow the man, imagining a fabulous relic only the privileged had gazed upon, not the usual bone or tooth or bit of cloth. His enthusiasm was contagious, and Magda, too, began to anticipate a miracle.

At the gate to the crypt, the guard turned and motioned them in. "You come," he said in heavily accented English. "You bring your wife."

Harry looked quickly at Magda, but her face showed no ripple of objection. Her features were soft in the dim reddish light reflected from the rose marble walls and ceiling. The black statue of St. Andrew towered over them, his hands raised in blessing. From one, dangled two fish of dull silver with ruby-encrusted eyes that flickered wisely. Harry stared so intently the fish appeared to quiver, their silver scales grown suddenly brighter. As he leaned toward Magda to confide the trick his eyes had played, the slight disturbance in the air carried with it a hint of oil from her hair.

High above them, out on the coastal road, arches cut in the cliffs mirrored the Gothic arches in the crypt. Like giant gates they opened on the blue skies visible through them where anyone could imagine angels dancing to the music of the spheres.

They descended many steps to reach the Grotta dello Smeraldo, which they entered through a dark mouth. Overhead the rock was ribbed like the ceiling of a cathedral, and all around them stalagmites rose like steeples. Harry took Magda's hand to help her into the small, overloaded rowboat that would take them deeper into the cave. Everyone spoke in hushed voices as if this were some holy place. The guide chanted his story in a deep baritone that echoed off the walls as he explained in Italian how one formation resembled the Madonna draped in a fine shawl and another evoked Mussolini. Magda only understood the words *Madonna* and *Mussolini,* but Harry leaned closer to whisper translations about the shawl and other details she could not make out. The only other sounds were the oars dipping into the water followed by their echo.

The boat paused above a life-sized ceramic Nativity submerged several meters but as visible through the clear water as if it were displayed above the surface. Christ sprawled in His cradle and Mary looked solicitous. Cows with wise faces slept with their thin legs folded beneath their bodies. The guide spoke of the miracle of Christ's birth as reverently as if it had happened right here in this cave.

Past an outcropping of rock, light from no apparent source illuminated the ordinary seawater now alchemized a rare emerald green. To reach it Magda had to lean across Harry who had an outside seat. Pressing her chest against his thighs, she dipped in her hand as far as she could reach. This must be the kind of light people who had died described when they were revived, she thought, a consoling light that compelled them forward before they were ushered against their wills back into the harsh, unholy light of daily life. The boat turned toward the rickety wooden pier. Righting herself, Magda touched her wet fingers first to her forehead and then to each breast.

When she settled back into her seat, Harry's legs felt suddenly cool. *La sposa*, he murmured, leaning into her to repeat the guard's mistake she had not corrected. In Italian he continued to whisper as if he were merely repeating the guide's remarks, but the words were ones he had no right to say.

Only because Harry insisted, Magda agreed to forgo Capri and rest for a day in Sorrento before the drive to Rome. Their daily excursions had repeatedly returned them to the hotel too late for leisure, and now he did not want to be on a schedule. They agreed to spend the day apart and meet in the lobby for dinner.

Waking late, Harry spent the remainder of the morning in his room customizing his hatband with a row of coats of arms he had copied from the cloisters at Amalfi into a tiny notepad he now carried in his breast pocket along with several drawing pencils and the zinc oxide. He made preparatory sketches and transferred them to the band in pencil before coloring them in with felt-tip pens. Some represented the major cities such as Milan and Verona, and others stood for the noblest families in Italy, the Medici and the Orsini. There was an eel, a bear, twin roses, a dove holding an olive branch, a dragon, three leaping dolphins, a winged lion, an oak, a lily, three hunting horns, and a serpent devouring a child. In the center, on impulse, he added a skull and crossbones. When he was finished, he put the hat on his head and admired his reflection in the full-length mirror on the back of the closet door.

That afternoon he took his pencils and sketchbook down to the hotel pool where he stretched out on a chaise longue he dragged to a shady alcove by the fence. Most of the women were nude and either slept in chaises or clustered around the pool to dangle their legs over the edge. Some were middle-aged and others were young with high, round breasts. Harry imagined them as Roman women on holiday in the baths at Paestum, lounging in the caldarium where willingness enveloped them like steam. When he appeared in the doorway in a yellow toga, they shrieked in mock alarm, then gathered around him, undressed him, and rubbed his body with fragrant oil.

Before long, Magda in a blue one-piece bathing suit wove between the rows of chaises, chose one, and turned it directly into the sun. He watched her drape her towel across its back, then walk to the diving board. Her dive was graceless, he thought, but she swam with ease underwater, drawing up her brown legs, then parting them and snapping them together to propel herself across the bottom.

Surfacing, she turned on her back and floated with arms outstretched, gravity free in the salt-water pool. She looked up at the flawless sky and the slow-moving branches of the orange trees heavy with fruit. Each breath she took echoed in her ears; magnified, it drowned out the chatter of the sunbathers ringing the pool. She closed her eyes for a moment, wishing she could sleep on water.

When she opened them, she saw Harry. He was wearing walking shoes, chino pants, a striped shirt, and his hat. His reading glasses sat low on his nose and he peered over the top at a cluster of women off to his left and then back down through the lenses at the sketchbook on his lap. He did not appear to notice her. She tried to determine the precise direction of his gaze because she wanted to know which woman he had chosen to draw.

Swimming to the ladder, she pulled herself up out of the pool. Channeled by the curve of her spine, water rushed down over her buttocks, thighs, and calves. The rivulets braceleted her ankles, traversing the small sharp bones visible beneath her skin. She spread out her towel and lay still, waiting for her breathing to slow. The sun warmed her like it did on the island beaches where she had lain beside Ramon before they both became too aroused to either read or sleep. Slowly she eased her bathing suit down around her waist. Harry glimpsed her breasts before she rolled onto her stomach and shut her eyes.

Flipping to a fresh page, he sketched her as she lay, thinking past muscle and bone to the slow contractions of her heart. He heard it beat in his ears: two beats, a soft one followed by a louder one that confirmed it, like a woman murmuring *yes* and *yes*.

Back in his room he filled in the details he had not lingered to complete. When he was finished he took off his clothes and studied himself in the mirror. Again taking up his sketchbook, he added himself to the drawing.

Although he had sat in the shade, Harry had sweated through his shirt and would have to shower before dinner. He had barely enough time, but he would hurry. The tiny, windowless bathroom in his cramped room was barely larger than a coat closet. One step put him directly in front of the toilet. The bidet on his right jutted out to meet it at a ninety-degree angle, and a sink the size of a soup bowl protruded from the wall on his left. A shower nozzle arced out over the fixtures and drained into a slot in the center of the floor.

Turning to throw his towel on the bed to keep it dry, he struck his shin on the toilet bowl. He swore lightly, pulled the door shut, and turned on the cold water full blast. Eyes closed, he waited for the shock. Finally a thin stream trickled down over his shoulders. He soaped up, knowing the pressure would increase when he mixed in the hot. He worked the lather into the thick hair on his chest and underarms. For a moment he thought of Magda, imagining her luxurious bathroom with celadon tiles and a platform supporting an oversized claw-foot tub just his size. Right now she was probably soaking in that tub. He stifled a pang of jealousy. When the image returned, a new, playful Magda reclined neck-deep in bubbles like Marilyn Monroe posing for a calendar shoot. Soaping his groin, he felt the beginning of an erection.

Harry was annoyed with himself. Pressed for time, he resented the distraction. In spite of himself he replayed the scene: tile floor, claw-foot tub, one leg in and then the other—Magda's, he knew—toenails painted with red polish he added as an afterthought, a stomach several shades whiter than the rest of her body, and breasts he did not have to imagine. Gradually he focused on her nipples, their plum-colored areolas dimpled as if from a chill. Reaching into the picture, he cupped her breast and took the nipple between his thumb and forefinger. In his mouth it was a nub like the eraser on the tip of the pencil he sucked from time to time while he sketched. Both hands were on his erection, working the foreskin down over the head and quickly pulling it back. Leaning against the bathroom door, he came in his hands. When his breathing slowed he opened his eyes, and everything was the same as it had been before.

He turned the spigot marked *caldo* but instead of the rush of hot water he expected, the trickle of cold gradually diminished and then stopped. He spun both handles back and forth but nothing happened. The lather on his chest and in his crotch began to itch. After a few more minutes of fiddling, he washed off the soap as best he could in the tiny sink. Magda would be waiting.

The doorknob he turned slipped under his hand and failed to catch. He stepped back in surprise and then jiggled the knob and pushed, but the door did not budge. His breathing accelerated and a fine sweat broke out across his forehead. Clenching the knob in both hands, he pulled. The toilet shuddered under his sudden weight when he fell back on it, the doorknob in his hands. He sat for a moment, panting, surveying the knob as if it were a curious artifact. This is not a crisis, he told himself, merely a delay.

Searching the tiny room for tools, he found a discarded razor blade behind the bidet. He used the blade like a credit card, forcing it between the jamb and the door. Somehow he was not surprised when it snapped. He held up a sliver the size of a fingernail; the rest had fallen through the crack. Sweat stung his eyes and trickled down between his shoulder blades. He pictured Magda in the lobby checking her watch, trying to decide whether or not to call his room. The telephone rang. He counted the rings. There were twelve before it stopped, and then it started again as if she refused to believe he had not answered.

His eyes darted around the room and settled on the toilet. He lifted the tank cover, hoping he could dismantle the ball cock and use one of the parts to pry open the lock or pick it. A glance confirmed the rusted screws and metal tubes were useless. With a quick gesture that surprised him, he bashed the ceramic cover against the spot where the knob had been. The door quivered under the insult. He moved to hit it again but was overwhelmed by the sensation that his antics were being observed by an amused, white-coated attendant calmly taking notes behind a one-way mirror. Suddenly he was concerned with appearances, of being tested and found wanting, of being judged by an unseen eye — cool blue like the blue part of Magda's eye. Like hers it stared down at him but itself remained inviolable.

The voice of reason again manifested itself. *I am not a brute*, he intoned to himself. *There is no eye in the sky, and I will not be defeated by a bathroom door in a backward country that can't print a clear road sign.* He lunged at the door with his shoulder. The impact sent a dull shock down his spine that jarred every bone. The door bent slightly outward then stabilized. He lunged three more times in quick succession like a thug in a gangster movie. On the last try the wood splintered and the door swung suddenly open, catapulting him onto the bed headfirst. He was free, but there would be damages to pay.

Magda waited a long time for Harry. She telephoned his room, but he did not answer. She telephoned again, and again he did not answer. She checked with the desk clerk, intending to ask if the man in room 29 had gone out. She knew only two of the words she needed: *uomo* and *ventinove*. Apologetically she framed her request, filling in the spaces with English. The clerk looked puzzled. No, Magda decided, he would have to be clairvoyant to understand.

She returned to her straight-backed lobby chair and continued to wait. He would come; she knew it. Closing her eyes, she wove a bright thread that traveled across the lobby and out to the hotel's terrace and garden then back to the bar, through the restaurant, and into every corner looking for him. At each juncture, it paused and swiveled like a periscope, but no Harry appeared on the empty horizon. Finally she concluded he must be in his room. His heart rattled in the cage of his ribs. She heard it. He was having a heart attack, the result of too much sun, too much fried fish. And now he was alone on his knees in a tiny room with no one to save him and without having seen Rome.

Guilt overwhelmed her. He had been good to her, he was selfless, kind, he knew things for which she had given him little credit, and he had watched out for her. All this she had repaid with senseless arguments, provocation he had not deserved. He was dying, and now she was sorry. She saw him in his coffin, his face in sweet repose. He wore his Stetson and his nose was coated with cream from the little tube tucked into in his breast pocket. Those things she had ridiculed she now found endearing.

Reality suddenly intruded. In spite of her grief, she would have to make funeral arrangements. Where would he want to be buried? Would he want a religious service? What denomination? Would he prefer cremation? How could she plan all this with the words *uomo* and *ventinove*? She needed him to make these arrangements. She could do nothing without him.

When she reeled in the bright thread, Harry came with it. He stood in front of her, in the flesh, sheepish as a cat that had misjudged the distance to the windowsill. Joy argued with regret. Of course she was glad he was alive, but she had already rehearsed her comportment at his funeral. "Yes," she would have whispered behind composure's thin veil, "we were traveling companions," but her voice would have hinted at more.

Harry nudged her ankle with the tip of his shoe. "I was afraid you'd leave," he said.

X

FOR HARRY, ROME WAS WEALTH AND POWER, KNOWL-
edge to be processed and absorbed, all on a grand scale, kingly. All that he admired frustrated Magda. She complained there was too much of everything—too many streets, churches sometimes side by side, palaces, fountains, obelisks, too much art. It was impossible to find anything in the singular, anything small enough to hold in your hand.

When he coaxed her out of the hotel that first day, he toured whole districts while she remained in a single church photographing the saints limb by limb. Then she sat in a back pew, enjoying, she said, the serenity while she waited for his return. She would not venture out alone. Even armed with guidebooks and maps, she knew she could not find her way.

"Trust your instinct. All roads lead to Rome," Harry teased.

"But I'm already in Rome," Magda said, refusing to be cajoled.

"I only meant that you can't get lost. One street leads to another and then another, and soon you're back where you started."

"Maybe that's the problem. Maybe I want to arrive somewhere instead of walking in circles until I drop." This was something Harry could have said, Magda realized, after a day spent trudging through the Valley of the Temples or the labyrinthine streets of Pompeii.

Harry showed her how to hold the map to orient herself. "All you have to do is read the street signs, check them against the map, and then turn left or right," he said.

"Most of the streets don't go left or right. They veer off or twist and divide in ways no map could ever show. No, you're on your own," she said, insisting their system worked: Harry would see Rome and she would become intimate with a few newfound saints.

The next day he took in the colosseum, the Roman forum, and the Palatine Hill where Romulus and Remus were suckled by the she-wolf. He stopped often without Magda, for a beer or to engage in conversation with anyone who loitered—an old woman sitting on the curb repairing her shoe, a man who had stepped outside the shop where he baked pizzas over an open flame, a bus driver out on strike. They were willing to talk and appreciated his eagerness to absorb whatever they knew: the routines of their daily lives, a colloquial expression, where to go for good, cheap food. By the end of the day he felt more Roman than tourist.

Santa Maria della Vittoria was a small church, but the hours passed quickly for Magda who had not spoken one word aloud. In a glass case beneath a side altar lay the wax body of the saint for whom the church had been named. She wore a shimmering gown with stars and crescent moons outlined in glitter. Her head was propped at an odd angle on a small embroidered pillow to display her slit throat and the three tear-shaped drops of blood issuing from it.

In an alcove off to the left, St. Theresa swooned in ecstasy. A boy angel lifted her toward the Heaven she sought, her habit hooked between his thumb and forefinger as if they alone could pull her out of this world and into the next. In his other hand the angel held a gold arrow with a sharp metal point.

Although her body was draped in voluminous marble folds, the curve of her shoulder, the line of her hip and thigh were still defined. Yes, she was a saint, but she was also a woman. Magda shot close-ups of her parted lips, her closed eyes, the bare foot that dropped off the stony ledge adrift like an earthly cloud, and the toenail the master had carved on the tip of each jointed toe. Photographing the foot balanced on a ridge as sharp as a razor blade, Magda remembered how Bernini had worked in a trance, requiring apprentices close by to prevent him from stepping off the scaffold into thin air. He, she realized, like St. Theresa, had tested the restraints of this world.

It was the arrow that interested Magda, for it was the catalyst that would transport St. Theresa through the long tunnel of pain and see her out the other side. Only after many photographs did Magda perceive the direction of the arrow, how it angled down toward St. Theresa's pelvis. It was a dirty trick, she thought, a sick joke that reduced holy fervor to a bizarre sexual act, confused the sacred and the profane or, even worse, equated them. She went outside to wait on the steps for Harry. Beside them she noticed a sharp stone the size of a pea. Taking it up, she pressed it into her palm and closed her fingers tightly around it. Without untying her right shoe, she wedged the stone down into the hollow between the ball of her foot and her heel.

Harry saw her sitting on the steps before she saw him. Hunched over, fiddling with her shoe, she looked like a child waiting for her mother to pick her up after school. Eager to report the events of his day, he called her name and waved. Rising to meet him, she stepped down hard on her right foot. Before they reached the corner she linked her arm through his. Later she leaned on him, for she had begun to limp.

Harry dallied on the way back to the hotel. He said he wanted to shop for souvenirs. Every shop showcased replicas of Romulus and Remus straining toward the wolf's teats. Floor-to-ceiling shelves were crammed with statues in every conceivable size lined up nose to tail. After visiting a dozen shops, Harry finally decided on several small reproductions in alabaster before he began looking at the larger ones in bronze that required two hands to lift.

Taking down a statue the size of a loaf of bread, he set it on the counter beside the others and asked Magda what she thought. She watched him run his hand across the wolf's back and down under her belly to the eight conical teats, heavy with milk. Although the wolf's fangs were bared, she had kind eyes. She stood still and let the fat babies squat beneath her, heads tilted back, mouths open to receive the streams of warm milk that would direct them toward the men they would become.

As a girl Magda had found two black kittens, the only ones in the litter to survive after their mother died. On her father's workbench in the garage, she fashioned a bed of towels and then searched the neighborhood for a cat with babies of its own. Dragging it home, she nestled the kittens she had found up against the cat's nipples. They had barely begun to work their tiny mouths before the cat, profound in her indifference, stepped over them and jumped down off the bed. The kittens tangled in her legs cracked their heads against the concrete garage floor, mewling and jerking. Shortly afterward, they both died. That's how hard it is, Magda learned, to accept anything into your life you have not always called your own.

Magda told Harry she understood his fascination with the abandoned babies who would have died if it had not been for the wolf that found and nursed them. It was the kind of miracle all lost souls hoped for as they searched the forest of daily life for succor made more miraculous because it came from a source so unlikely.

The shopkeeper wrapped the statues in tissue and Harry arranged them in a white plastic bag he hung over his arm like a basket. The handles cut deep into his arm from the weight.

That night Magda dreamed she held a map flat on her palm. Spinning the map slowly, she tried to match up where she was with where she wanted to go. She watched as Via d. Umilta became Via d. Dataria and Via d. Muratte became Via d. Lavatore or Via d. Stamperia, depending upon which branch she followed. In her fist she clutched the two coins she would throw over her shoulder when she found the Trevi Fountain. The sound of rushing water convinced her the next street would open out onto the piazza where Ocean rode in his chariot drawn by matched pairs of seahorses and tritons.

A tiny side street tempted her with its charm but it ended abruptly against a stone wall. Again and again she turned the map to find herself, hoping for a gold arrow pointing to the words YOU ARE HERE that would direct her to a place she could call home. Without warning the net of thin black lines became rushing streams, erasing the street names and dissolving the map she tried to catch as it slipped from her hand.

Slowly the walls of the city closed in on her, pressing her into a corner where the only meaningful direction was up. She leaned back against the cold stone and let her eyes travel to a patch of blue sky overhead. Yes, she thought, she would make her first wish now. She would wish for a hand to descend, lift her up, and set her down in some safe place. Unclenching her fist, she saw the coins were not coins at all but two sharp stones that had cut deep into her palm.

First she felt his breath on her neck and then the electric hair on his arm after she turned toward him. A hat shaded his face. On the map he laid on her open palm, the streets were marked with a clarity she believed divine. She looked up at Harry with gratitude, for it was Harry, as she had suspected all along.

When she touched him, his body was damp with sweat. Only then did she realize he was naked. She touched each of the eight nipples on his chest, and then her hand began to drift toward his groin. She woke to find her hand between her legs. Magda remembered she had one wish left, and it was to leave Rome at once.

Harry wanted to spend the day at the Vatican. "It's a city," he argued, "no bigger than Ravello or Positano, places you liked. And they have maps. Millions of tourists follow those maps and see everything they want in just one day."

"It's still Rome," Magda insisted.

"Of course, but it's walled off, like a separate place." Harry emphasized each syllable by striking the edge of his open right hand against the palm of his left as if he were building a miniature city. "Nobody spends just two days in Rome," he continued. "It's criminal. People make pilgrimages to this city. It's a holy city." He described the great dome of the Basilica di San Pietro that housed the black statue bearing the likeness of the saint, its right foot kissed smooth as glass, and the obelisk in the Piazza crowned with a relic of the holy cross. "And that's not even a fraction," he concluded.

She did not look at him while he talked but rather at her rings, which she twisted back and forth. Finally, she said, "Listen, I want to see those things too, everything you said. But I can't stay. It would mean a lot to me if you'd trust me."

"No questions, no answers. A leap of faith, that's what you want. You know it's too much to ask," Harry said.

"Yes, but I am asking, and it's hard for me to ask."
"All right," he said at last. "But I'll want something in return."
"What?" she asked, startled, looking up.
"Something. Not now, but soon."

XI

IN THE WALLED CITY OF ASSISI, MAGDA AND HARRY walked in the footsteps of the saints. They started at the cathedral of San Rufino where St. Francesco was baptized with St. Chiara, his mate in sainthood. The font stood in a dark corner. Harry leaned over the railing that instructed tourists to keep their distance and touched the marble rim. Magda studied his fingers, thinking he was feeling his way toward a sketch he would complete in his room that night. When she followed suit, she did so to invite those on the other side to touch back; not the saints, of course, who were busy, but Ramon, circling the earth alone, unlike Paolo who clung to his Francesca even in death. The rim under Magda's fingers was cold, unyielding, and she withdrew her hand.

Later, in the church of Santa Chiara, they saw St. Francesco's tunic of rough, undyed wool tattered beyond ordinary wear, hanging in a glass case reinforced with iron bars. Beside it rested his talking crucifix and the breviary whose pages he had turned. St. Chiara's embroidered surplice hung companionably nearby. In Italian, Harry read the placards that told the story of their long relationship and then translated for Magda who was more enchanted by the lively syllables released into the air than by the rigors of spiritual love.

"Do you think they were lovers?" he asked at last, returning his glasses to his pocket.

"I'm sure they loved each other, the saints loved everybody. They had to."

"As man and woman?" Harry asked, refusing her evasion.

"There wouldn't have been anything like that. They took vows, like priests. But they could have loved from a distance," she conceded, "like Cyrano, who loved but was still pure."

Harry glanced at her, but he could not intuit the deeper meaning he felt certain she intended.

Following the signs that read *Eremo delle Carceri*, they drove out through the olive groves to the hermitage where St. Francesco walked and prayed. The road wound through forests of oak and cypress then stopped abruptly in a cul-de-sac at the top of the mountain. Leaving the car, they walked the path through hills traversed by streams and dotted with caves where the brothers of the Franciscan order had lived. Some were marked with hand-painted signs. *Grotta Fra Leon* one read, but its mouth was barred and locked. Overhead the oaks arched into a canopy. It was here where St. Francesco preached to a gathering of doves and the wolf lay tame at his feet, where the cricket sang to him and hopped into his hand when he called, and where the skylarks rose in unison at the moment of his death to escort his soul to Heaven. Harry knew all those stories, and they held no less fascination for him now than they did when he had learned them as a boy in Sunday school in Ohio. In the hermitage he felt himself in the presence of a kindred spirit, as Magda would have said.

On the path Magda watched Harry pick up rocks in interesting shapes split from centuries-old boulders and put them in his pocket. When they stopped beside a crude altar fashioned from a stone slab balanced on a pedestal, he laid out the rocks like the pieces to a jigsaw puzzle. First he selected two small oval stones and carefully spaced them at the center of the slab. On them he rested a piece of shale that looked like a robe hanging in folds. Before Magda's eyes a figure began to take shape, its arms raised in benediction. With a flourish Harry added a thick triangular stone to form a head covered with a hood that draped onto the shoulders. A shaft of sunlight flickered through the trees, setting the figure in motion. "St. Francis come to life," said Harry, waving his hands like a magician's.

Delighted by the effect, Magda photographed the figure and the slab, but not the pedestal. The twigs and sprigs of grass she arranged in the background would look like trees in the developed slides. In fact, the miniature saint Harry had assembled would look like a full-grown man emerging from a forest and walking out onto a vast bleached plain. When she was finished, she gathered up the stones and tucked them into her camera bag.

The tiny church hollowed out of rock where St. Francesco had worshipped was deep in the heart of a group of attached buildings that had been built up around it. To reach the church they wound down a narrow circular staircase hewn from rock and walked bent over through tunnels barely five feet high. Harry was afraid his girth would force him to turn back without seeing the church. Squeezing through sideways, he still scraped his stomach. Even Magda could not navigate these passages with ease.

The church was a cave so small it barely accommodated the two of them. An altar filled one wall, and above it there was a high window that lit the cave with natural light, although Harry could have sworn they had tunneled deep underground. He had not planned to kneel in the dirt where St. Francesco had knelt, or close his eyes, fold his hands, and pray to embrace all things without reserve or judgment. On the blank screen of his closed lids, he saw himself climbing the thick rope of goodness hand over hand. Then he felt Magda's shoulder against his as she knelt beside him, and he wondered if she also prayed and, if so, what prayer she conjured in her heart.

Harry led the way back out. He stood near the opening of the small dark tunnel where Magda, who had lagged somewhere behind him, would emerge. When she did, he first saw her hair burnished by the sun, curls fanning her head face like a halo. Her eyes, when she looked up, did not focus on him but rather at a point beyond him; her gaze was so intense he turned around. Although he thought he had read recognition in her eyes, he saw nothing behind him except the familiar sun-drenched oaks.

They took a different route back to Assisi. Fields of sunflowers turned the landscape into a yellow sea parted by the dusty road. The flowers were brilliant, their immense round faces turning imperceptibly to follow the sun.

In the Hotel Subasio Harry was not surprised that his room was on the street side, alive with heat and the sound of engines straining as they climbed the steep hill leading to the basilica. Directly below his window was a stoplight that regulated traffic entering the walled city, allowing cars first from one direction and then the other to pass through the gates single file. After the tourists were settled in, the concierge had told him apologetically, the delivery trucks would run all night, carrying their heavy loads of supplies to the hotels and restaurants inside the walls.

Magda's room overlooked the valley where the tiny white houses nestled into the land's gentle roll blinked like earthbound stars. The slatted doors opened onto a large terrace bordered with flowering trees in blue ceramic pots and a decorative wrought-iron fence. "It isn't fair," she agreed, but secretly she appreciated whatever it was in the Italians that privileged women in this particular way. Harry could not imagine actually falling asleep in his room but said he would try to rest.

Dozing fitfully between the traffic's starts and stops, he dreamed of a fine villa fallen into decay. Although its owners were long dead, someone had sculpted the shrubs on the vast grounds into an elaborate zoo and mowed a broad swath of fragrant grass to form a path Harry followed to the veranda. Four tall columns rose on each side of the double doors. When he tugged on their heavy brass rings, the doors resisted and then gave way without warning. He saw at once that the facade was all that was left of the great manor. Beyond the doors lay a jungle overgrown with crawling vines, azaleas sprouting immense magenta blossoms, fruit trees of every kind, and wild flowers in profusion.

A speckled goose strutted past, leading Harry to a chain of islands flung like leaves across the weedy lake. On each island a different species reclined, some among the boulders, others beneath the solitary palm, always male against female, for there were two of each. They were drowsy, at ease: lions, zebras, camels on their knees, slow-eyed water buffalo, parrots with startling red and green feathers, flamingoes craning their necks toward him, pelicans, peacocks rattling their open fans like castanets, slack-jawed alligators, sea turtles, and long pink snakes draped like vines among the fronds. Their faces were wise and did not startle when they saw him dressed in a rough, brown robe. He held up his hands to reveal a bloody wound marking the center of each palm. They nodded their understanding. Slowly he lowered his hands and waded into this peaceable kingdom.

Harry was still groggy when he left his hot, traffic-soused room after midnight. Making his way away from the fumes and roaring engines, he found himself on the back of the hotel where the public terraces spanned its length. One level above them was the row of private terraces reserved for the now darkened guest rooms. Lights flickered in the valley behind Harry; ahead of him a spill of boulders banked against a retaining wall and planted with flowering vines connected the two rows of terraces. He saw the boulders as steps ending at the wrought-iron railing outside Magda's room. The stairway to heaven, he joked to himself. The doors she had pointed out as hers were open but as he watched they drew closed, pulled by an invisible hand. He felt a quick sensation of loss, as if something that had been his were suddenly wrested from him.

Although they had looked navigable from below, the boulders were steep, slippery, and too far apart to afford easy passage, Harry discovered as he began to climb. On the ground he had imagined himself swinging up like Tarzan and dropping on Magda's terrace with no visible trace of exertion, but Tarzan had not worn chinos that bound at the knees and crotch. Pausing at each hard-won plateau, he hitched up one pant leg and then the other, always sure to keep one hand on a rocky edge. The swarms of mosquitoes he raised with each gesture buzzed in his ears, but his hold was too tenuous to slap at them with conviction. He let them sting him.

Balancing on a boulder near the summit, he groped along the terrace's cement edge to locate a fence post he could use to pull himself up. When he swung one leg over the railing, he felt the seams of his trousers strain. He crept over to the doors and knelt in front of them. With one ear pressed against the slats, he listened for several minutes but heard nothing. Closing one eye, he squinted with the other as if framing a difficult shot with his camera, but the slats angled sharply upward revealing only more slat. He stood on his toes and dropped down on his hands and knees, but still he could not see into the room. Overhead, the restless wings of the night birds cut with ease through the summer air.

What was he waiting for? he asked himself. Did he expect the doors to swing magically open like the stone rolled from the mouth of Christ's tomb? And what miracle would prompt Magda, half drugged with sleep, to rise and embrace him, saying, *My hero, come at last,* even though she slept so close he could hear her if she murmured the answer to a question someone asked in her dream.

And what did she dream, he wondered, behind her closed eyes? If he made up a dream for her and thought about it hard, would the course of her dream shift as easily as a scene framed by the window of a passing train? Impulsively, he pressed his lips against a wooden slat. It was rough as a beard, not smooth like the foot of St. Peter enthroned, the foot he had neither seen nor kissed. He did not know how much time passed before he rose with effort, crossed the terrace, and descended by the same precarious route he had climbed.

Back in his room, he opened the shutters and looked out at the basilica in the distance bathed in welcoming light and at the street below where the trucks labored like Sisyphus with his stone.

Sweaty, streaked with dirt, Harry slowly unbuttoned his shirt and scratched at the bites swelling on his neck and arms. All night they would itch. By morning the crisp white sheets would be flecked with his blood.

XII

THE DISTANT TOWERS OF SAN GIMIGNANO ROSE FROM the hills of Tuscany like obelisks. Thirteen remained of the dozens that families had built to show off their wealth.

"It's like a fairytale," said Magda as they drew closer, "towers fit for princesses. They could dream at their windows, waiting to be rescued."

In Siena she had seen a fresco of a little castle town set on a hill. A man decked out in armor and a gold cloak with black diamonds spilling down the side rode across the foreground on a white, high-stepping steed dressed to match. How effortlessly he could carry away a maiden in distress. The guidebook said he was a famous Sienese general, but Magda preferred to think of him as a knight.

Harry, who knew some history, said, "The families who built those towers were at war with each other. They'd haul rocks up to the top and stone anyone who looked at them cross-eyed."

"Come on, Harry, would it hurt to be a little romantic?" Magda chided.

"I can be a lot romantic, but I didn't know you cared," he said in the voice he had learned to enlist like an alternate identity, as if he were not responsible for anything it said.

"Oh, I care," she said quietly, smoothing her skirt down over her knees. In another woman the gesture might have been coy, but in Magda-of-the-high-collars-and-long-dark-skirts it was as demure as a nun adjusting her habit.

For once Harry had no reply. Besides, his neck was hurting again from too much driving. As soon as he parked, he turned his head sharply to one side, cupped his chin in his palm, and pushed until his neck cracked. The sound was like stone striking stone.

Across the piazza, the facade of the Chiesa di Collegiata was humble, unassuming, even dingy. Inside, the church was small enough to take in at a glance. Turning to leave, Magda was startled by the frescoes that covered the walls high on either side of the doors. The guidebook had made no reference to the scenes from Bartolo's *Last Judgment* that flanked all who entered. The souls of the damned languished in darkness on the left. Satan enthroned rested one horny foot on the backs of kneeling sinners, and the flailing legs of others protruded between his jagged teeth. Around him cavorted the minor devils with sleek black skin, double sets of horns, and sinuous tails. Given free rein, they choked the men, disemboweled and decapitated them, then gave them back their heads to hold in their own two hands. The women they raped and sodomized with swords or flaming torches. One devil rode a woman like a horse, pulling back her head with fistfuls of her hair while another squatted on a ledge above her and shat into her screaming mouth. When the women tried to cover their breasts and genitals, the demons pulled their hands away and led them off with snakes looped around their necks like ropes.

"Brutal," said Harry.

Magda hardly trusted herself to speak. She felt the humiliation of the women depicted on the wall. For her the fresco had come to life like a scene in one of those books that animated the figures when the pages were quickly flipped. She heard the bones crunch like Harry's when he cracked his knuckles or neck, and her cheeks burned with a sensation that traveled in waves down her body. Without stopping to look to the right where the souls of the saved flourished in Heavenly light, she left the church.

Harry followed her out to the piazza. Men lounged in every doorway or played cards at small tables they had brought outside. Aviaries fashioned out of screen were fitted into the windows of the second-story apartments and dozens of canaries fluttered inside.

Catching up with her, Harry guided Magda to an outdoor café and a table with a blue umbrella that shaded them from the sun. After a while, he took the notepad from his pocket and sketched the small fountain in the piazza's center, a simple sculpture of a dolphin cast in bronze with water spurting from its open mouth.

Looking at her over his glasses, he handed her the drawing. "For you," he said.

"It's a wonderful gift," she said, noting how he had embellished the simple design, endowing the dolphin with sturdy splayed feet and enormous wings to make it capable of traveling any terrain. After a pause, she added, "I could give you a gift."

He touched her hand lightly to encourage her to continue.

"I could give you the answer to the question you didn't ask when we left Rome," Magda said, holding his gaze.

"He's been following us," Harry blurted out before she could continue. "I've seen his car." As soon as he said it, both of them became aware of how much had passed between them unspoken.

For Magda, Harry's admission released a torrent of words she had suppressed. "I don't know what he wants. We spoke only once but he seemed to know everything about me, or maybe he made it up and convinced me it was true. I've dreamed about him. It's crazy but sometimes I think I hear him at night outside my room. It would mean nothing to him to put his shoulder to the door and break it down." Breathless, she sank back into her chair.

Harry thought of himself as she spoke, how relentlessly he had watched her and how he had knelt outside her door. It was as if she had spliced together segments of two different movies, one starring the dark stranger and the other starring Harold D. Bagnovich, although the story was seamless.

"I meditate to try to learn where he is," she continued, again leaning forward. "It's something I do. In Rome his energy was strong. He was there."

"And in Sorrento," Harry added, "at the festival."

"He stayed at our hotel to spy on me. Even if I didn't see him, I could feel his eyes on me. In Rome it was different. The energy was crazier, demonic. He was like a dog at my throat." Magda shuddered, laying her own slender fingers against her throat, the diamonds in her ring glinting like tiny teeth.

At last she had privileged him with a confidence, and he felt a rush of sympathy for her as one who had endured a private sorrow without consolation.

Impulsively, he rose from his chair and kissed her cheek, one chaste kiss. Reaching up to take his face in her hands, she searched every feature for the answer to a question she had not fully framed. Whatever she found permitted her to cup his jaw and turn his face from side to side, kissing first one cheek and then the other. "Like the Italians," she said. The bristles of his two-day growth pricked her palms, but she merely pressed them harder against the stubble.

XIII

"*Lago,* LAKE. *Lago di Garda,* LAKE GARDA," SAID HARRY, and Magda repeated the words after him. Overnight, it seemed to her, Harry had sorted through his Portuguese, Spanish, and Italian, cataloguing and separating until he had become fluent in all three languages. In Florence and Milan he had met Brazilians and Spaniards in banks and hotels, coincidentally, she thought at first, but then she understood that they recognized one another, as if they were members of a secret sect.

He had talked his way through northern Italy, solving problems of travel that stupefied her. She regretted her obstinacy, her wrongheaded preference for the shallow sounds of the English she spoke with little intonation, barely moving her mouth. Harry, like the Italians, spoke with his whole body, gesturing vigorously as if to draw up the active syllables that tumbled from his lips like monkeys. Now she, too, wanted to learn.

The lake was sheltered by the Dolomites and the mountain chain of Monte Baldo. Nestled down among them, fed by cold mountain streams, the district had been a resort since Roman times. Travelers from all the dirty pigeon-infested cities of Italy retreated to these shores, and here Magda and Harry would rest for a week before returning to Milan and the flight home.

The clerk handed Magda the key to room 220 and laid the key to 221 on the counter. Magda took both keys and when Harry returned with the luggage, she gave him the key the clerk had meant for her. 220 had a bathroom the size of their bedrooms in Rome and an adjoining balcony that afforded uninterrupted views of the lake. The tub was long and deep and stood on a raised platform. 221 also had a balcony, but a row of tall pines obscured the lake and the bathroom was an afterthought with no tub at all. "At last," said Harry, "a hotel in Italy where men are privileged." She hoped he would offer to trade rooms so she could decline, but he did not. She never told him about her small sacrifice.

Finally, she admitted to Harry, she had no need for her camera bag, for anything it contained. Setting out without it she felt lighter, like a runner who jettisons his weights on the day of the big race. After their first day of hiking in the crisp mountain air, they were both giddy. When they returned to the hotel the power was out, but they laughed over this slight adversity and stopped in the bar, which was lit with red candles in holders. It was festive, they agreed, over the bottle of Bardolino they shared. They jostled their way up the dark stairs and down the hall to their rooms. Unlocking their doors, they each flipped the light switch and then remarked upon their foolishness. Such creatures of habit they were.

When it became clear there was no back-up generator and they could expect no power for hours, Harry went back to the bar, snuffed out several candles with his fingertips, and smuggled them out in his pockets. He knocked on Magda's door and presented two of them to her with great ceremony, describing how cleverly he had cadged them after being told at the desk that candles were at a premium and they were unable to supply their guests.

Harry took his candles to the bathroom, filled the tub with hot water, and opened the balcony doors, admitting a burst of chill mountain air. Sinking down into the near-scalding water, he looked out at the mountains and listened to the lake lapping against the retaining wall below. When the heat became intolerable, he rose dripping from the tub and went out on the balcony, bracing himself against the shock. Back and forth he went. *Caldarium, frigidarium,* he thought, just like the Romans. Each time he rose, the candles cast his shadow on the wall, immense and wavering. He kept up his regimen until the water and the air were the same temperature.

Dressed in his pajama bottoms, he returned to the balcony bare chested. He stood there only a few minutes before he heard Magda's balcony doors open. She stepped back quickly into her room when she saw him.

"Come on out," he called. "It's great out here."

"I'm wearing my nightgown."

"So? I'm in my pajamas. Well, part of them."

Magda hesitated then folded her arms across her chest and went out to join him. "The candles are nice," she said, "but it's still too dark to read. My mother used to take my books away because I read by flashlight under the blankets at night."

"You look like one of your princesses there on the balcony, but a knight would have to use a boat to rescue you," Harry said, changing the subject.

"Or I could fly off on the dolphin you drew for me," replied Magda, recalling its jointed wings.

"Can you see the lake from there?"

"A little, but I can hear it. It reminds me of an island I know."

"A vacation?" asked Harry. "Hula skirts and all that?"

"No, the Caribbean. A tiny island no one visits, not even me any more."

Looking over at her, he remembered her on other balconies as a distant figure he had glimpsed, and he remembered her as he had imagined her behind doors she had shut in his face. These scenes aligned themselves on memory's white wall like a series of paintings that portrayed the same subject in different light.

Now here they stood, her in a nightgown he had known would be white, and him half dressed. They were close enough to join hands if they wanted to.

"Magda's an unusual name. Is it a family name?"

"My mother was Catholic. She named me Magdalene, hoping, I suppose, that Christ would drive the devils out of me, too."

"Lots of people are named for saints, but I've never known a Magdalene."

"I'm Magda now. It's legal."

In Florence Harry had photographed Donatello's bony Magdalene, a gaunt-faced, wooden figure draped in rags, matted hair framing her tortured face. But he had also seen Titian's painting, a nude-to-the-waist, full-breasted Magdalene, a sensual dream-touched woman whose rosy flesh would retain for a moment a depression left by a fingertip. Harry saw his Magda in both artists' visions.

Everything Harry had learned about Magda he had learned by accident, watching and listening without appearing to and filling in the blanks with educated assumptions as in *Rome, Past and Present*, a book he had bought that showed the crumbling foundations and stumps of the occasional pillars on one side and the missing pieces sketched on a transparent overlay on the other. Completion was a matter of turning the page.

"I've never liked my name either," said Harry, "but I suppose everyone wishes they had a different name."

"Harold is a good name. I think of *herald* with an *e*, a messenger, a harbinger, an angel with a golden trumpet."

"No one calls me Harold. I'm always Harry, and there's a little too much truth in that," he said wryly, running his hands over his bare chest.

"I believe we grow to fit our names. If you change your name you can change your life."

"Is that how it worked for you?"

"Yes," she said, for her life had changed. It had been full until her losses began to eat away at it. Now her name stuck in her throat like a bone. That was the difference it had made, the single syllable severed from her name. "But it's a story I never tell," she added. "Besides, it's not one story but a story that leads to other stories."

She could hardly explain how she saw her life as a freight train with boxcar hitched to boxcar or how she stood separate from it, waiting at the crossing for it to pass. One after the other an endless chain of identical cars lumbered out through a wall of black smoke. Metal gnashed against metal as the train labored past in slow motion, blocking her view of the open sky beyond.

"I've got time," said Harry, leaning forward and resting his elbows on the railing.

Magda watched the clouds drift and imagined them mirrored on the lake she could hear but not see. The sound was evidence of its presence, but to believe it was there still required some small act of faith.

"Sometimes I see things," she began. "I did it on purpose as a girl. It was like travel, getting away for awhile. But then, like dreams, they took whatever direction they chose."

"Good dreams?"

"At first."

The waves were steady as a metronome.

"There was a man who looked like me," she continued. "I loved him, and then he died. It wasn't fair."

Harry felt jealousy prick him. When he tried to imagine the man she had loved, he saw only a larger Magda with short hair. But for her Ramon materialized in an instant on the dark-haired firs that blocked her view; it hurt to look. She had loved him, although she had not loved herself. Skilled at abandonment, she had quit herself and moved inside him. Maybe she had forced him out.

"At first I tried to call him back. He didn't come. And then I went to him."

"You tried to kill yourself?" Harry asked softly.

"No, nothing like that. I traveled." After a long pause she added, "But I could not find him." These words hardly described how she had risen out of her body and looked down on the world, searching for the spot where he lay. She had to cross an ocean to find him. Like rain she entered the earth, but it was dark and shadows twisted into grotesque shapes warned her back. When she did not listen, they let her see how the earth opened to a bottomless pit where horned demons with rapacious mouths tortured the lost souls who entered there.

Harry moved to the corner of the balcony closest to her and pressed against the railing. He framed questions that she answered before he asked them.

"I never went back again, but I never stopped calling either. And now he's here."

"When you love someone, that person is always with you," said Harry, thinking how he had carried her in his heart.

"It's not like that. He found his way back. I got what I wanted, but it's different. He crossed over. He used to be a good man."

Harry studied the line of her jaw in the clear blue light. He knew she believed what she said. Influenced by some combination of desire, fairy tale, and a misreading of *The Lives of the Saints*, she concluded she had willed her lover back to life and that he now inhabited the body of the man they had first encountered in Palermo.

"Magda, listen to me. I know what you mean. I know what it's like to want something so badly you convince yourself you have it. When longing is that strong, it's easy enough to be tempted... that's how hard it is to accept that you cannot have what you really want." He could not bring himself to confess, even if it would console her, how many times he had woke from his dreams bitter with regret, cursing the loss of something he had never had.

When Magda gave no sign she had heard him, he swung one leg over the railing. He straddled it for a moment, feeling the cold metal between his legs. Waves sloshed against the rocks below. The two balconies were farther apart than he had thought, and he could not cross from one to the other without risk. For a moment he considered the hallway, a knock on her door, but he feared she would not answer or the spell would be broken and she would politely explain her fatigue. Besides, his leg over the railing committed him. He struggled to suppress the vertigo that began as a slight numbness in his extremities, a wavering behind the eyes, a tightness in his scrotum. Gathering himself, he crossed the strip of air between them. There was a split second when neither foot was secure.

At another time Harry might have joked about coming to the rescue of a maiden in distress. Although it was hard for him to admit it, he now understood what drew the knight to the tower. It was the curve of resignation in the posture of a woman of goodness and beauty, her plaintive voice, and the knight's own refusal to believe there was nothing he could do, his inability to walk away brushing one palm against the other. No, it was not a matter of being a romantic as he once had argued.

Her shoulder was thinner than he had supposed, the bones sharp and angular. When she did not object he put his other hand on her back and pulled her toward him, fearing for a moment she would become suddenly aware he held her.

She moved into the small circle of his arms and pressed her forehead against his cheek. Foolish, mapless, Magda felt as if she had spent her life wandering to arrive at some destination she could neither recognize nor call by name. The word *arrival* was itself a cruel misnomer.

The two of them stood as if on a shelf between the vast blue plain of the lake that stretched to the horizon and the cold dark stone of the hotel. Small as dolls posed in each other's arms, what gesture, what phrase could possibly make a difference?

"I'd like to hear you tell yourself another story," said Harry, "a brighter one. You chose before and you can choose again."

As if from a great distance Magda saw the wall between their two rooms dissolve and their rooms become one long room. Intricate moldings rimmed the ceiling and framed the row of tall windows. Reflected in the glass, she saw the moon in all its phases lit by a spinning sun, Saturn's glowing rings, belted Jupiter adorned with its ruby spot—these last flanked by the smaller planets, each bearing its name emblazoned in stars. The twelve signs of the zodiac outlined a zodiacal man—the ram draped across his head with horns rising like a crown and his feet resting on two kissing fish. Constellations of the northern and southern hemispheres circled at will: the winged horse; Cetus, blunt-nosed as a whale, tail coiled like a dragon's up over his vestigial wings and forelegs; the lyre, delicately strung as the good ship Argo's rigging; and Perseus joined to his wife, Andromeda, who balanced one foot on his raised sword.

Such a sky held all knowledge, charted or intuited, every creature, known or fantastical. To look upon it was to be a god. And there was a god in this heaven, enthroned on a sun held aloft by myriad angels who sang the music of the spheres. On his right hand the spirits of the apostles wavered and on his left they inhabited their earthly guises. The saints opened their arms in welcome, and the blossoms they walked on were not crushed but nourished by their feet.

Then there were the seven seas that rose and parted as if commanded by the rod. They flaunted coral reefs studded with shells. Moray eels nosed out of the crevices, and stunning parrotfish hung as if suspended from a mobile. The floor was rippled from the bottom currents, and mountains and valleys rose and fell like waves. For each of the seas there was an attendant continent, and the tawny land sprawled like the bodies of women who slept in peace.

But, in truth, there was no separation between the elements: every entity was replicated in sky, sea, and land. Hydra, snake of stars, uncoiled across the sky with the same motion as the eel and snake of the sand. And what, after all, was a wing if not a fin, a hoof if not a foot? They were as similar as object and shadow. To know one was to know the others. This is what Magda would have understood in the cathedral at San Gimignano as she stood in front of Bartolo's *Last Judgment* had she looked at the frescoes on both sides of the door.

When the vision paled, she felt no sense of loss, for she had taken it in. From a distance she had seen what surrounded her, what had been within her reach all along. Turning back to herself, she hovered for a moment above the woman on the balcony, and then she slipped down inside her.

Magda was as weary as if she had traveled a great distance on her knees, like a penitent following the maze cut into a cathedral floor. She folded her hands, fingers interlocked. Squeezing, she became aware of the rings she had worn so long she rarely noticed them. The rough-nubbed diamonds and sapphires marked her skin with their pattern, the x of something crossed out, null and void. In the dark, they could be bits of ordinary stone or the thorny heads of cloves; but if she held her hand to the light, the gems would assume depth and luster, they would reveal their value.

She squeezed again. She could make them hurt like a bad memory. No wonder she imagined them arcing out over the waves, and the two nearly inaudible plinks they would sound before they sank. With her right hand she turned them gently then twisted hard until they cut into her knuckle. They barely budged. It was as if they had attached themselves to her finger like mussels to the side of a tide pool. So what if she cast them out into the water? Fish bait or buried in silt, they still claimed their few centimeters somewhere in this world. And anyway, what assurance did she have that such a loss would become gain?

Turning away, she went inside and lay down on the white sheet. When Harry sat beside her, the linens puckered under his weight. She did not look at him but rather at the creases that verified his presence. Perhaps she slept. When she opened her eyes he was still there, leaning forward with his elbows on his knees. She did not know how much time had passed, only that he had remained, watching over her as if he could protect her from herself. When he rose, the sheet still held the shape of his body.

The candles had burned themselves out and in the moonlight Harry saw only her suntanned face and arms; the rest of her had disappeared in the white nightgown against the white sheet. Leaning over her, he took the hem of her nightgown between his thumbs and forefingers and eased it up to her hips, which she lifted. The dark shape of her body, revealed in increments, seemed conjured from air. When he bunched the gown above her breasts, the white band of fabric made her head look as if it had somehow floated free. He thought of the lake, how it blued, paled, and blued again. Laid out on the sheet she presented herself as a dichotomy, a choice: her mind on one hand, her body on the other. And her heart, he wondered, where would he find it? Adrift in the gauzy absence between the two?

He slipped off his pajamas bottoms and lay down beside her. When he moved to touch her breast, she caught his hand and returned it to his side.

"Look at me," she whispered, "I want you to," but he could not see, as she did, burned into her lids the dark face of the man who had known her body as well as his own.

For the two years since his death, Ramon had hovered above her like fog and her reach had yielded empty air. She had known him in the past and would know him again in the future; only in the present did he remain unreachable. Listening to the steady pattern of Harry's breathing, she thought how, in such circumstances, one man sounded much like another. When his hand drifted toward her again, she let herself be touched.

Harry felt her quicken, although he sensed a measure of reserve, something held back. He had waited through weeks of polite conversation, dinners across tables, separate rooms, obstacles strung up like arrows and released into his flesh, obstacles he had not surmounted but had waited out.

Privately he had suffered, suppressing desire and its attendant rage. Like a dog trained to the hoop, he now came forward for his reward. It was not all that he wanted, but it was more than he had; he would settle for what she could give. When he guided himself into her, her eyes moved behind her lids.

Harry had spoken of choice, and Magda had chosen the only way she could. He had been sent as a messenger, an intermediary, a stepping stone on the path that would join her world to Ramon's. There was risk, of course, and there were consequences. Although Magda knew the story of Orpheus who had journeyed against all odds into the world of the dead, she did not think of it now. Like him she had tried to bear her loss but could not, and like him she sought one who had been taken too soon. Orpheus had charmed the three-headed dog with his song and returned to the bright world with his heart's desire.

There the story should have ended, for at that point it contained joy and grief enough. With humility Orpheus had obeyed the edict that he must not look back. Tempted though he was, he did his part. Only when he was safely out of the cavern's dark mouth did he turn to find Eurydice still robed in shadow. It was a miscalculation, a senseless hitch, and for that the highest passion was repaid with loss.

The tongue that filled her mouth tasted as bitter as her own bitter tears when Harry's face came into focus, even though she had not opened her eyes. All stories were finally the same story—hers, Harry's, all the Magdas and Harrys past and future—and this was the story: woman of sorrow, woman of ecstasy, they were the same woman. Pain pricked her to the quick, as it did the souls of the damned in flames who looked across the abyss to beflowered Heaven. For Magda, like them, there was pleasure in glimpsing such grace, in knowing it was possible, although not hers.